The critics like Keith Hale:

The real triumph of *Cody* is its portraits of adolescent love. This reviewer can think of no recent novel which has done it better . . . Keith Hale has the gift of crafting scenes and setting down spot-on adolescent conversation with its peculiar humor and conveyance of much more than what is actually said. *Cody* . . . is a very considerable achievement.

—Frank Torey

With this refreshing presentation Keith Hale has emerged to stand along with the current "new wave" of gay writers. Top of the heap of gay fiction.

—Thomas Hopkinson
Gay Community News

Cody

A novel by
KEITH HALE

Alyson Publications, Inc. • Boston

Published as a trade paperback original by Alyson Publications,
40 Plympton St., Boston, Mass. 02118.
Distributed in the U.K. by GMP Publishers,
PO Box 247, London, N15 6RW, England.

First edition: April, 1987.

ISBN 1-55583-105-2

Author's acknowledgements:

Thanks to Robert Lowe for his help with preparing the manuscript, my parents for providing the room in which I typed it, and Sasha Alyson for publishing it. Thanks also to Phil Revels, Dave Corbett, James Grauerholz, Until December, and Cheri Koch. For their help in Amsterdam, thanks to Frank Torey, Peter Glencross, Mark Watkins, Leo de Kam, and Sander Van de Bilt (for one perfect kiss).

Cody

One

I was staring at the boy who sat diagonally in front of me, about five feet away. Mrs. Kraemer was lecturing about the Cold War, causes and effects, and around the room students were half-listening in case they were called on, but mostly daydreaming, for this was the first day Little Rock had been without rain in over a week, and the sky had turned a wonderful, swimming blue.

Since Little Rock had only recently become my home, I'd been going to this school for less than two weeks. Being "new boy" was a role I had become familiar with, however, as I'd attended almost a dozen different schools in half a dozen towns over the last eleven years. Still, it was a role which always made me uncomfortable, especially when it came to making friends.

For three days I had stared, discreetly from the corner of my eye, at a certain boy in class, but had not gathered the courage to speak to him. I had chosen him primarily through instinct, but also because he looked good, seemed cheerful, and showed remarkable intelligence when answering or posing questions in class. He was forever challenging the teacher on points of historical interpretation, usually presenting the best argument. Unfortunately, he seemed oblivious to my presence, making me apprehensive about approaching him.

Mrs. Kraemer was discussing the democratic elections which Russia had promised to hold in the East European countries after World War II, but which either "were never held at all or were not what we would call democratic." I knew all of this from my own reading, since history was a subject I had always found fascinating. It was even reflected in my name: Trotsky. Actually I was Steven Trottingham Taylor, and thus far had allowed teachers to call me Steven or Steve, not knowing how they would feel about having a Trotsky in the classroom. But I had been called Trotsky all my life by those who knew me best, and that was the name I intended for any new friends to call me. The name meant a lot because it was a sort of memorial to my father, John, who had been a union organizer back in Milwaukee until he was shot to death during a strike in Chicago. My mother, pregnant with me at the time and left with naming me herself, waited to see what sex I would be, then named me Steven (my paternal grandfather's name) and Trottingham (her family name), having it in her head that I was to be called Trotsky.

The sudden realization that I was being stared back at jarred me into averting my eyes. But I had been caught, and now the boy was looking back every few minutes, smiling once or twice, but more often eyeing me with a mixture of curiosity and suspicion. Mrs. Kraemer noticed he was being distracted and asked him crossly exactly what *he* thought of the Russians.

Cody — for that was his name — was not often caught off guard. With just the slightest hesitation he answered in a clear, earnest voice, "I hear they speak well of our revolution."

Amid scattered laughter, Mrs. Kraemer pondered his answer. "You mean the American Revolution, I presume?" Cody indicated he did, then explained his answer less flippantly:

"I believe they respect our revolution as a great example of the proletariat rising to break the chains that enslaved them, but they feel we went wrong somewhere down the line and allowed a class system to enslave us once again."

Several students objected loudly to Cody's statement, and for the first time in this class I offered my own comments, suggesting the Soviets might do better to criticize their own revolution, since it had gone wrong in the eyes of many when Stalin wrenched power from Trotsky and his followers.

My statement restored order immediately, since hardly anyone — including Mrs. Kraemer — seemed to know what I was talking about. Cody gave me another look, with a bigger smile than before, and offered that he could agree with my assessment. Mrs. Kraemer then hurried us into the Berlin crisis so she could give us her prepared homework assignment before the bell rang: If you were John F. Kennedy, *what would you have done?*

Indeed, what? When the bell rang for lunch, I was disappointed to see Cody hurry from the room with another student, undoubtedly having plans. Although I had hoped he wasn't so popular I would have a hard time making his acquaintance, I could not imagine him being unpopular. He was too self-assured, knowing how to make the most of what he had. Disturbingly enough, he appeared to have everything — charm, wit, good looks, and intelligence. The only thing missing, perhaps, was money.

I assumed Cody was about my age — seventeen. Of medium height, he was well built even to the point of being somewhat muscular, with broad shoulders and slim torso. His face was as smooth as a child's — it was obvious he didn't have to shave — but something about his cheekbone and jaw gave him an aura of underlying toughness and kept him from looking boyish. Cody's eyes were a soulful blue, but it was his hair that eclipsed his other physical attributes in commanding attention. Cut in layers, it hung over his collar and frequently over his eyes, flopping up and down in lively, radiant strands when he walked. But the color was the most intriguing aspect — sort of orangish, but not exactly, close to blond, but possessing the more attractive elements of auburn and brunette as well. As for clothes, Cody came to school practically every day wearing a plaid cotton shirt, worn jeans, and tattered tennis shoes, giving the impression of being as close to the earth (and to poverty) as you can get without dying — natural to the point of intimidation, in that you wanted to look the same. At least I did.

It was raining again by the end of the day, a thunderstorm having appeared from out of the west. I pulled my windbreaker close around my neck and with a finger freed that section of my hair which had been trapped between neck and jacket. The sky had darkened to a point where the street lamps were beginning to buzz themselves aglow, and the rain coming down through their glimmering light gave me a calm feeling of presence. The city seemed strikingly deserted, as if rain were in fact enemy bombs and everyone had taken shelter underground. Although the shops were still open, the only person I saw on the streets was a policeman making out a ticket for a Subaru which had been cleverly squeezed between parking spaces.

I had begun looking for a job as soon as school was dismissed at 3:30, setting out on this quest without much planning, encountering nothing more than frustration. Every place I tried either did not need anybody or found me lacking in experience. One store manager told me my hair was too long and they were primarily interested in hiring a woman.

"A short-haired one, I take it," I said on my way out the door.

Soon after it began to rain I abandoned my search, at least for the day. I was feeling what all young souls must feel when they attempt to enter the job market, wondering how I would ever find work if it all required the experience I did not have. Now, standing in the light, steady rain, I had quite by accident come upon the Arkansas State Employment Service. Realizing they would soon be closing, I quickly walked inside, pleased to find it, like the streets, deserted.

The receptionist provided forms to fill out, said I should perform this task quickly, and instructed me to wait for an interview. All this in one breath and without so much as a glance from the papers over which she was huddled. She could have been a recording, but I imagine she knew this, and I doubt that it bothered her.

The form was easy enough to complete, except for providing a mere three spaces for listing the dozen or so schools I had attended. I could only remember the addresses of three, anyway, so I listed those and invented three sets of "dates attended" totaling eleven years. Next I was required to provide the addresses at which I had resided over the past ten years, and again there were three spaces. Totally inadequate, the spaces and I — my mind went as blank as the forms. Staring, evaporatively, at the furnace in the corner of the room, I heard my name being called. The receptionist still did not look at me but gave accurate directions to the proper desk.

Sitting at this desk was a girl about my age, perhaps a year or two older, whom I proceeded to study with a mixture of curiosity and awe. There was something about the way she was dressed, in a manner rather dashing, almost daring — certainly not something Arkansas women were wearing in that particular day and age, although it had not escaped my attention Arkansas women in that particular day and age were consistently given to overdressing for every occasion. I guessed it had something to do with being the forty-ninth most prosperous state for all those years.

The young woman, however, looking as if *she* were from another day and age, was talking to an older woman, and seemed to be ending a joke.

"And then the Mother Superior said, 'You smell like stale camel piss.' So the little sister went to wash up. When she returned, she asked, 'Do I still smell like camel piss?' And the Mother Superior said, 'Yes, but at least it's fresh.'"

The older woman did not laugh. "That is terrible," she said flatly, dropping a stack of papers on the desk to prove her sincerity. The younger woman tapped a pencil against her typewriter four times, contemplating, then shrugged. She was about to resume typing when she became aware of my presence, apparently for the first time.

"Who are you? What are you staring at?" she asked. The

tone in which she asked these questions was not especially unpleasant. It was the questions themselves which I found distressing.

"Uh, nothing. I mean you. No, uh, my name's Tro—"

"Well, can I help you?"

"Yes. That is, I think so. I wanted—"

"You're wet."

I recognized the line from a well-known cult movie, but I could not tell if this girl was trying to be funny or serious. She had said the words like an accusation, just like in the film. I recalled that the proper response was, "Yes, it's raining," but chose to make no reply.

"Sit down, but don't lean back," I was instructed. Then, seeing the forms in my hands, she added, "Give me those."

I had no opportunity to surrender the papers, however, for she had grabbed them already, only to quickly fling them back at me.

"These are *not* complete."

"No, um, I'm sorry."

She had the pencil in her mouth, apparently studying me. Really, she was quite attractive. Her personality had taken me by surprise, but I did not find it distasteful. It was almost . . . fun. In fact, I found myself waiting with uncharacteristic anticipation for whatever she would say next. She seemed quite content with making me wait, even though closing time was fast approaching.

The pause gave me a chance to regain my composure. I scanned the desk, hoping to find a nameplate buried somewhere beneath the rubble. Even an extraordinary creature such as this was sure to have a name. I was in luck, spotting the familiar, wooden, triangular prism with a golden plate on one side and green putt-putt golf felt on the underside, only partially covered by the pile of application forms. Her name was Sarah Turner, a name which seemed unnervingly wrong. I had expected Cassandra Constellation maybe, but not Sarah Turner. It was even spelled with an 'h'.

Sarah Turner, meanwhile, was offering me her pencil, pointed end first. I accepted it. The eraser was wet from having been in her mouth, an intimacy which pleased me, as did the teeth marks scarring the wood.

"You might finish those now," Sarah suggested, indicating the forms.

"Yes, I might."

Sarah had things to do, so she did them while I labored over the forms. Then, once again, she grabbed them.

"Amazing," she said.

"Pardon?" I smiled, no longer nervous in her presence.

"Oh . . . nothing," Sarah said, taking time between the two words to purse her lips and give me a questioning look. "What type of job are you looking for?"

"Well, I don't know, actually."

"I thought not." Sarah made a motion of dismissal. "The woman by the window reads palms. Why don't you give her a try?"

I glanced at the woman indicated, who looked more psychotic than psychic.

"Look here! I came for assistance in finding a job, and all I get is, is, some attitude!"

Sarah pulled herself up even straighter in her swivel chair, dug through a drawer, and produced a rubber stamp.

"I will try to set up some interviews," she began, "although in your case it may be difficult. Can you be reached at this number?"

"Yes. After school."

"Very well. Give me two or three days. Meanwhile, try to stay dry."

She began stamping away at the forms like mad. I watched as several sections of my handwriting were obliterated by the ink. Yes. Right. Well, she had to read the blasted thing, not me.

I got up to go. She did nothing to detain me.

In the rain again, I could not put the strange creature out of my mind. It was crazy to think I actually liked this alien, yet I had been sorry to leave — and for what other reason?

The sky had become even blacker than before; the rain was falling harder. I loved these dark skies and wet streets, and was even curiously attracted to a dark, wet, young man who eyed me uncertainly as we passed crossing the street. By the time I reached my car the rain was coming down in sheets. "Beautiful," I said, barreling into the rush-hour traffic. "Fantastic," I said at the first stop light. "Sarah," I said, plowing through an intersection filled with water.

Having no intention of relying on Sarah to find me a job, I spent the next afternoon in downtown Little Rock checking out leads from the *Arkansas Gazette*. One ad read, "EARN $1000-$3000 A MONTH. MUST BE ABLE TO TALK AND WALK." It seemed like very minimal qualifications. I assumed it was selling door-to-door, and therefore didn't bother to call.

Little Rock was unsettling. I had lived in the northern part of the country most of my life, but my mom had decided to move south because of the "better business climate." She always said that phrase as if quoting someone she truly loathed. Expecting to get a job as an economist after earning her master's at the University of Nebraska, she had ended up accepting an offer to teach economic theory at the University of Arkansas at Little Rock.

I had liked it okay in Wisconsin. It was those few years in the wheat belt I had hated. As for Arkansas . . . well, I was not at all sure. The culture seemed an odd mix, too undefined to be detestable, but too vague to appreciate. Also, there was something about not being a native Arkansawyer I could never get around, neither with the neighbors, nor at school, nor during my painful job interviews. But I had met only two of the neighbors, had been at school less than a week. Perhaps things would change.

Back at my car, I wondered what to do next. Despite the outrageous price of fuel, it was almost a relief to discover my tank was near empty. For the moment it would give me a sense of direction, of barely-affordable purpose.

On several occasions I had been tempted to stop at a station near my house, but had no excuse for doing so until now. What had tempted me was ... Cody, whom I had spotted working the pumps.

I was relieved to find the prices at this station relatively cheap. Seeing no one on duty, I went inside to locate an attendant, this station being one of the few left in town which had not converted to self-service. I heard a rustling sound coming from the men's room, and soon Cody appeared, holding a concrete pipe. It was a nice piece of concrete.

"Aren't you in my history class?" he asked. Thinking it would be insulting if he didn't know the answer himself, and remembering his leaving class without an introduction, I chose to say nothing. When he realized I wasn't going to speak, he looked at me through remarkably blue eyes sunk behind a marvelous, golden tan, and apologized for keeping me waiting. "What can I do for you?" he asked finally.

I kept my thoughts to myself, and said, "Fill it up with regular." It was the kind of thing one said at service stations. It was precise and to the point. It did not tell the attendant, "I think you're beautiful." It was merely instructional, the kind of thing one said to any attendant, beautiful or not.

I followed Cody outside to my car. "You could have been robbed," I said without inflection, thinking even as I spoke how trite it must have sounded.

"Even service station attendants gotta use it sometimes, and I'm the only one here."

This was true, leaving me nowhere to go with the conversation except, "I suppose they do," which seemed inane, but again, it was out.

"Would you like me to check your oil?" Cody asked.

"Yes, please," I answered, knowing I did not need oil, but also aware that Cody's offer was unusual, even for Arkansas.

Captivated by his hair, I silently recalled the opening stanza of a poem by A. E. Housman:

Oh who is that young sinner with the handcuffs on
    his wrists?
And what has he been after that they groan and shake
    their fists?
And wherefore is he wearing such a conscience-striken
    air?
Oh they're taking him to prison for the color of his hair.

"It's full," Cody said.

It was, I realized, time to pay and leave, but in absence of other customers, I decided to pursue an introduction.

"Your name's Cody, isn't it?"

"Yeah. What's yours?"

"Trotsky."

Cody almost laughed. "You must have some ridiculous given name like me. I get called lots of things."

"Yeah? Like what?"

"Well, my name's Washington Damon Cody, which lends itself to a lot of silly nicknames — The Demon, Codeine, Washington D.C. — but my friends call me Cody."

"That's a good name for you. I'm usually just called Trotsky, but my full name is Steven Trottingham Taylor."

"Doesn't Mrs. Kraemer call you Steve?"

"Yes — it doesn't matter much what teachers call me."

"Why are you called Trotsky, anyway?"

"Well, my mother is from an old English family — the Trottinghams — and my dad was something of a socialist."

Cody laughed. "Better be careful who you say that to around here."

"I don't notice you being too careful. In history, I mean."

"I take my chances," Cody said, with some incredible roguish expression crossing his face.

"You present some good arguments."

Cody thanked me, then went to service another customer who had driven into the other gas lane. "Guess I'll see you around, at school," Cody said, just before asking what he could do for his new customer, who I would learn later was actually an old customer, one of many who stopped in regularly for "three or four dollars worth," and invariably stayed a while to talk, creating a minor traffic jam around his two tiny gas islands. For others also found Cody extraordinary — everyone from adolescent girls to old-timers who had lived in the neighborhood all their lives, had watched this incredible-looking child grow into something between a boy and a man. But Cody understood their fascination even better than they did, and had long ago learned how to handle them.

When I returned home, my mother was holding the telephone to her breast, yelling, "Trotsky, it's for you."

This was the first call I had received in Little Rock. When I took the phone I simply said what most people say — "Hello."

"You ass," came the reply, "I've been calling all day."

"I'm sorry. I was in school." I had immediately recognized the voice as Sarah's.

"Listen, I've arranged an interview for you on Monday, four o'clock. Can you make it?"

"Sure. What is it?"

"Be there at four o'clock sharp. And wear dry clothes."

"Be where? What's the position?"

"You're to be interviewed by one Miss Whistle. Try not to blow it."

"May I please know what the hell I'm being interviewed *for?*"

"For a Clerical Assistant II position, Steven. I hope you like the title."

"Call me Trotsky. What the hell is it?"

My mother, walking by folding a dish towel, frowned at my language. Sarah apparently shared her view.

"Profanity becomes obscenity when fed with repetition, Mr. Taylor."

I had to pause for a moment, but even then could think of no appropriate rejoinder.

"It's with the phone company — one of the few places you

can get a decent paying after-school job in this town, as well as one of the few places still hiring during this 'mild recession.' Any objections?"

"I'm not sure."

There was a long, somewhat humorous lapse in conversation. Realizing I would have no excuse to contact Sarah again if I got this job, I decided to issue a challenge:

"Why don't we go out tonight and talk about it?"

Sarah made some funny animal sound which vaguely resembled a gasp. "Don't you have anything better to do?" she asked in a strangely hoarse voice.

"No. Where do you live?"

"I'll tell you, but I can't go out tonight. I've got to prepare for a party I'm giving tomorrow. Then a pause. "Why don't you come?"

"To the party?"

"No, silly, to the preparation. Of *course* the party!"

"What kind of party?"

"A string bean and Jello party."

"A *what?*"

"Just kidding. It's a party to celebrate a weekend of freedom. I live with my parents, who are blessing me by leaving town for the weekend. That only leaves my older brother, and he has plans, too. So . . . well, it will just be friends. I doubt if you will like them, but come anyway — I'll be there."

It was altogether tempting.

"Okay. Give me directions."

I threw up my arms and fell backwards on my bed, thinking of Sarah, then of Cody. Then of Sarah. Then of Cody. Then I turned on my stereo and went to take a shower.

Two

It was raining again as I drove my younger brother Freddy and myself to our respective schools, in the car Mom had given me on my sixteenth birthday. It was a fine car, never giving me any trouble except on cold winter mornings when it took a full ten minutes to warm up. An old Chevy, it wasn't old enough to be considered a classic. It was simply an old car. But it had endured the drive from Lincoln to Little Rock, and I wasn't about to complain. When it comes to material goods, I'm extremely easy to please. I liked my car, and I wished I could feel as contented in other realms of my life.

Freddy was in the ninth grade — junior high — and I was a senior in high school. At every traffic light I fought to pick my eyelashes clean of the debris which had stuck to them during my night of near-sleeplessness. What sleep I had managed I could call sleep only grudgingly, since every ten minutes I had opened my eyes to see if I was still awake. This morning I felt as if I were speeding; high-tuned nervous energy was at play on my fingertips, going in turn from eyelashes to steering wheel, while I maneuvered through a maze of sleepy Friday-morning people, most in their cars, windshield wipers flapping, exhausts exhaling, with some pedestrians in raincoats under umbrellas moving along at something between a walk and a trot. All of this I saw in blurs, when the rain was not too thick on the glass, when I was not staring instead at tiny black specks floating, I assumed, on my own cornea. Those black specks had always frightened me. I had mentioned them once to Freddy, who was relieved to know I saw them too. Always relieved, he was, we were, to find we were not the only ones.

Although very different in character, Freddy and I were close as brothers. He was the more sports-oriented, which was beneficial to us both, since Freddy's being so good in everything made it a task for me to stay ahead of him, even being three years older. There were many evenings and even weekends when we spent our time almost exclusively with each other, because we were there. That we had come to understand our differences long ago and were both basically good-natured, willing to compromise on almost any issue, was a blessing for which we both were grateful.

Of course, since my father was killed when my mother was pregnant with me, there's obviously another father in there someplace. Freddy's father was a man by the name of Benjamin Crawford. After three years in which he drove us half-crazy, Mom left him. I consider it good fortune that none of us, including Freddy, have seen the man since. When Mom moved the family to Nebraska she changed her name back to Taylor, and changed Freddy's name as well, since he wanted to have the same last name as Mom and I.

On the radio was a song I liked, partially for the music and vocals but mainly for the lyrics, which I imagined to be about the vocalist — a man — losing a male lover, although the song was actually genderless. I wondered sometimes if I was exaggerating the various clues in the lyrics, and I wondered absent-mindedly why I would want to do that.

I was in front of Freddy's school, but since traffic was at a crawl, he was waiting patiently until the car was at the point closest to the door he meant to enter. Freddy was at an age in which peer pressure ruled out carrying an umbrella, although if asked about it I'm sure none of his peers could have given a reasonable explanation as to why umbrellas were taboo. The car having reached its closest proximity to Freddy's choice of entrance, he said "See ya," and departed. My own school was not far away, but the traffic proved a sufficient obstacle to make me late.

I was forced to park far from any entrance, and there were two or three chutes of water racing down the pavement between my car and the school. I stepped out of the car with my books in hand and immediately raised my umbrella. A sudden gust of wind just as I was pushing it open caused it to double back in broken frenzy. Seeing no clear reason to own a convex umbrella, I threw it down in the parking lot and hopped back in my car. After waiting maybe four minutes for the rain to slacken, which it did not, I ran the fifty yards to a door, and into Cody, who appeared from 'round the corner. Cody cursed me good-naturedly, then held the door open as we both entered. There was something known as a hall monitor waving his arms in sundry directions, with instructions for everyone to go straight to class, late passes not being required on this occasion.

Facing the inside of my god-only-knows-what-shade-of-green locker, still breathing heavily from my run across the parking lot, I tried to remember what class I had first that day, rotating schedules forever throwing me into confusion of space and time. With some uncertainty I decided it was English, gathered what I thought I would need, closed and locked the locker, and walked slowly down the hall, now trying to remember if I had been given homework for English and, if so, had I completed it. I was surprised to see Cody walk into the debate room, since I had always thought debate classes did little more than teach students how to be socially annoying. With Cody, I supposed it might account for his ability to argue so effectively with Mrs. Kraemer about history.

Not until gym, my last class of the day on Fridays, did I see Cody again. I was fully changed into my white t-shirt, white shorts, white socks and white sneakers when Cody entered the locker room, surprising everyone. He nodded a greeting to me before several guys who apparently knew him pretty well grabbed his attention and kept it by demanding to know what he was doing there. From bits and pieces of the conversation overheard, I gathered Cody had received a schedule change and would be in our class. Though pleased, I wondered if we would still be in history together.

I walked to the gym floor and sank some baskets until everyone appeared for roll-call. During this ritual we had to sit on the bleachers and answer "Here, sir," whenever our names (our *sur*names) were called. This completed, we moved along to more strenuous exercises, such as side-straddle hops, knee-bends, and the infamous squat-thrusts. I would like to personally disassemble whoever it was who thought up squat-thrusts.

Since it was raining outside, again, volleyball was the sport of the day. Everyone in class, including the coach, seemed to know and like Cody. It didn't surprise me when he was asked to be a team captain, but it certainly shocked the hell out of me when upon winning the coin toss he said, "I'll take Trotsky." I wasn't the only one surprised. Nobody knew who he was talking about at first, since everyone knew me as *"Taylor!"* Then, when I stepped forward beside Cody, they all looked at me as if I were some secret weapon they had overlooked. But I proved a good choice for Cody, serving, in one of my better performances, for eleven unreturned points, picking apart weaknesses in the other team's defense. My teammates were all praise in the dressing room, showing for the first time some interest in getting to know me. I smiled and said "thanks" a few times while Cody sat next to me on the bench, undressing, not saying a word. Baffled by his silence, I tried not to glance at him. Only when Cody gave me a slap on the back on his way to the shower did I look up.

Freddy and I shot some pool later that evening, then watched television a bit before I left for Sarah's party. It was raining again, but by now I hardly noticed. Nothing could spoil my good mood, except, perhaps, that horrible smell coming from the Pine Bluff paper mills. I had been in the hospital once, the result of a childhood bike wreck in which I had tried to miss running over a frog, flipping my bike off a bridge in the process — and breaking my nose and my arm. (At the age of nine, I was awkward beyond my years.) Although both had healed back nicely, my sense of smell had never completely recovered. French cooking, for instance, was wasted on me since I could not detect the subtle aromas. Whenever I did smell something, the scent would often linger inexplicably for hours, sometimes days. It had been nearly three hours since the aroma of the paper mill had blown in on a strong wind from the south.

With Sarah's directions as accurate as the receptionist's, I easily found her house. A taller, older male with jet black hair and ivory skin — a strikingly effective combination — answered the door. Noticing his complexion was similar to Sarah's but carried a step further toward perfection, I knew this had to be her brother. Obviously on his way out the door, he pointed towards noise and said, "The party's in there. Enjoy yourself."

I looked him squarely in the eye and said, "Thank you. I will."

Some other creature with jet black hair, a dog, leapt at me from under a chair as I entered the medium-sized room. But Sarah had already dislodged herself from another guest and come to welcome me, looking smashing. Her hair appeared to be longer and blacker than before, her clothes more foreign and curious.

She introduced me to various groups of people — so many, in fact, that it was hopeless trying to remember names. Mother Nature was talking to us at the moment. I knew it was Mother Nature because she had apologized for the weather, after I had invited disaster by saying, "Hi. How are you?"

"Hi yourself!" Mother Nature spat back. "What do you mean, 'How am I'? You think I can answer questions like that? I might just as well ask, 'How are *you*?' I am madness. I am livid. I am Westernized to a greater extent than you will ever understand. I am a normal person whose head is hurting. And the weather's just horrid. And I *am* sorry." Then she was gone.

I knew immediately this was a drama crowd, and this in a

sense explained Sarah's strange appearance. As the night wore on I discovered any number of pretentious people: boys from Sherwood (the North Little Rock suburb, not the forest) with English accents, girls from Pulaski Heights who spoke in French as often as they spoke in Southern. Collectively they seemed to know all the lines to at least a dozen camp films, and they appeared not to care how many times they bored you with the same Mae West rejoinder or Tim Curry affectation. Sarah stood out simply because she was infinitely more subdued.

Mother Nature brushed by again to say "I really *am* sorry about the weather. Terrible moisture."

"So this is Arkansas humor in mid-September," I muttered.

"So this is mid-September humor in Arkansas," echoed Sarah. "You would think it was her party."

The party *was* pretty much hers. Sarah told me it had been Mother Nature's idea from the start; for the most part these were Mother Nature's friends. She was, equivocally, Sarah's best friend. Sarah did not especially like her, however. Sarah had few friends of her own, but a few of these had just arrived. One of them was Cody.

"Would you like another drink?" Sarah asked, after following my stare across the room to the new arrivals.

"I had thought you incapable of clichés," I responded.

Sarah led me into the kitchen for something better than what was being offered to the party at large. I started to protest on the grounds that I was a junior Socialist, but I wasn't sure I had actually made that decision, therefore I thanked her for the drink, which she informed me was a White Russian.

Sarah then led me down a dark hallway to her bedroom. The small room had navy blue carpet, light blue walls, and grey curtains that matched the bedspread. The decor appeared to combine the remnants of a young girl's fuzzy-bear collection with a more recently acquired taste for Parisian launderettes — there were clothes scattered everywhere. Sarah grabbed an armful from the bed and tossed them to the floor. She then sat down. Sipping from the drink, which really was quite good, I did the same. We studied each other, a bit suspiciously as it were. Sarah drew me closer, until my chest was pressed gently against her breasts.

I was more nervous than thrilled. If I went through with this, it would be the first time. I felt I could handle it, but wasn't sure. Sarah **was** actually vibrating to my touch, and I felt a bit guilty that I wasn't sharing her excitement.

I had no idea how to get those peculiar garments off Sarah's body. It would have been challenge enough with someone wearing normal clothes, but with Sarah's spacesuits, well . . . I suggested she do it. Sarah consented, stood up, and began to undress. When I started to do the same she stopped me, saying I should be content to watch for the moment. Then she stripped herself sensuously, but without decadence. I appreciated the performance as art, but not as erotica. Sadly realizing I was not excited about the prospects, I began looking for an excuse to terminate things. As if by providence, there was a crashing of bells or glasses and several screams from the other room, sounding sort of like Bette Midler being run over by an ice cream wagon. And soon there was a knock on the door.

"Where do you keep your mop?" a male voice inquired.

Sarah, apparently not caring to know the reason for this distressing intrusion, answered, "In the broom closet adjoining the kitchen. Like ninety percent of America, I imagine."

"Right," the voice said.

Alone again, I suggested that perhaps Sarah should investigate the accident. Sarah, in the nude, began to investigate the buttons on my shirt. Soon, too soon, she had removed it with ease and was working on my jeans. Just before she could discover that the erection she was looking for wasn't there, I stood up abruptly, grabbing my pants and snapping them back together.

"No," I said, with much difficulty. "I'm sorry."

I could tell Sarah was thinking about questioning me, but she apparently thought better of it, and with a sigh began to dress herself. I watched while trying to think of some excuse I might offer. I chose silence and felt oddly comfortable with the decision, especially since Sarah seemed to be accepting the situation.

As we left the room, she said quietly, almost off-handedly and to herself, "Why do all the best guys have to be gay?"

My initial impulse was to protest her interpretation of what hadn't happened. I opened my mouth to do this, but closed it again. When I did speak, I said, "That hasn't been my experience."

We had rejoined the party by the time I made this reply, and Mother Nature, walking by, paused to ask, "Well then whose experience was it, dear?"

To my relief she did not stand still long enough to demand an answer.

Cody came up next, made it clear he knew Sarah, then said he wanted to introduce me to some people.

"Everybody, this is Trotsky — he's in a couple of classes with me," Cody began. "And Trotsky, these are my two best friends, Christian and Flipping."

I exchanged greetings with each of them, noting that I had seen them both at school, although not in my classes.

Christian asked, "Doesn't Sarah frighten you?" but indicated he did not expect a reply.

"She's about as predictable as a bisexual tornado," Flipping muttered, drawing snickers from the other two, and a smile from me.

Mother Nature came by again, but before she had a chance to speak, Christian and Flipping both screamed at her, "*Will this ungodly weather never cease!?*" It was done with such perfect unison that everyone within earshot fell silent at once, then exploded in spontaneous laughter. While an upstaged Mother Nature engaged the others in a conversation about ferns, I took the opportunity to discreetly examine Christian and Flipping, a non-critical but earnest attempt to see what about them might attract Cody. My only guess was they seemed genuinely friendly and fairly bright, certainly not the worst of traits. It was apparent Cody did not choose his friends by their looks, and I felt good about that. Too many good-looking people insist on associating only with other attractive bodies.

Mother Nature changed the topic of conversation from ferns to a dog named Ralph. This mutt of indistinguishable breed had grown up in a pigpen. The dog, apparently thinking he was a pig, had become very neurotic when Mother Nature purchased him and brought him to the city. When Ralph was fixed with leash and collar, he created such a roar with his gasping and squealing that the neighbors would yell at Mother Nature, "What're you doing? You're *choking* that poor dog!" Ralph also had some intestinal problem, most likely from eating pig slop all those years, which became conspicuous through his habit of scooting ass-down across the carpet in circles, leaving brown streaks as he went.

Then Mother Nature toasted us and left, with Flipping, to get another drink, to toast somebody else. It wasn't until Flipping stood up that I realized how tall he was. His appearance when sitting gave the impression of someone considerably shorter. The only other physical features I noticed immediately were his eyes, which were those type of wide-apart, searching eyes that make otherwise common features seem attractive, and his hair, which was as long as any I'd ever seen on a male. He was wearing camouflage fatigues, and when he stood up Cody winked at him and said, "Don't shoot anybody."

With Flipping gone, I studied Christian. He had that color of hair I've often heard described as dishwater blond. He was even taller than Flipping, and extremely thin. His face was narrow and his eyes had a habit of darting around nervously in their sockets. Christian smiled a lot, and the common appeal of both him and Flipping was a nice contrast to the prohibitive beauty of Cody.

"Do you think your band's gonna get off the ground?" Cody asked Christian.

"It had better. If it doesn't, I don't know what I'll do. Except for a musician, I have no idea what I want to be, just a long list of things I *don't* want to be."

"I know what you mean. Most of the time I don't even

know what I want to do, just what I *don't* want to do. It's a feeling I've been having more and more over the last few years. But I know I want to travel, to see the Canyonlands, the moors of Scotland, frozen tundra. I have an intense desire to see frozen tundra." Cody looked at me. "Do you ever feel that way?"

"Quite a bit," I answered.

"That's why music is so important," Christian said. "It makes me feel good all over. Usually I feel so scattered."

"Music and roller coasters," Flipping added, rejoining us without Mother Nature. "I don't know which gives me more thrills."

I agreed with him. "Yeah, I'd like to take a transcontinental roller coaster ride from New York to San Francisco. Can you imagine what a trip the Rockies would be?"

They liked the idea. "I wonder why they spent their money on that silly railroad when they could've built a damn good roller coaster," Cody mused.

I learned quite a bit about Cody and his friends that evening. Christian and Flipping were involved in a band with a guy by the name of Stanley. Neither seemed to care too much for Stanley or his taste in music, but they put up with him because of his talent with drums and his ownership of their sound system. They admitted this, but weren't proud of it. Flipping played guitar and Christian played bass guitar and keyboards. Though everyone wrote songs, Christian and Flipping stated a strong aversion to anything written by Stanley. They discussed a new tune Stanley had pressured them to learn:

"The melody alone drove us both to smoke, but the words were just *horrid!*" Christian said. "He seems to have more rhymes per verse—"

"Rhymes perverse!" Flipping echoed. "That pretty well describes Stanley's songs all right!"

"At least we didn't have to hear him sing it. He's had mono all week."

"Maybe he'll make it up to stereo by next week," Cody said, encouragingly.

Christian apparently remembered he had just met someone who probably had little or no interest in conversations about Stanley. He turned to me and said:

"That's a very *Texas* shirt you're wearing."

I was wearing a faded blue work shirt with a single silver stud on each shoulder.

"As a matter of fact I got it in Texas this summer. We took a short vacation on the coast after moving down here. It's gotten slightly ripped, but I still like to wear it."

"Well, that makes it even more Texas."

"Yeah, I guess most Texans are slightly ripped."

Everyone laughed, to my pleasure.

"I've seen you at school. How do you like it so far?"

I shrugged. "Too early to know. Not much different from any other school as far as I can tell. A lot more integrated than any I've ever attended, but that's fine with me."

"All the white kids pulled out and went to private schools," Cody said.

"Not all of them," Flipping reminded him.

"Well, Milwaukee's hardly made a start at integration," I said, to everyone's surprise. "And in Nebraska there aren't enough blacks to matter."

Mother Nature, apparently having forgiven the earlier insult, joined us once again. With her were a young woman introduced to me as Val, and a slightly older male, probably in his late twenties, who introduced himself as Robert. Cody, who knew them both, later told me Robert was the only person he knew who had been officially declared stupid. A woman had asked a dating service to match her with someone handsome and intelligent. They gave her Robert. The woman sued the service, claiming that while Robert wasn't bad to look at, he was an airhead and she deserved her money back. The judge agreed.

"We went to a puppet show this afternoon," Robert said, apparently to Cody.

"What kind of puppets were they?" Cody asked. "Hand puppets?"

"No, um, gosh," Val answered. "I don't know what you call them. They were, like, puppets on a stick."

"Hush puppets," said Mother Nature.

"I haven't — gosh," Val began, speaking to me. "I mean, where are you from?"

"Wisconsin," I replied.

"Oh gosh! I bet that's really, um, cold. I don't see how people, you know, *survive* in places like that."

She said "survive," as if she were very pleased to have thought of the right word. Already, I was beginning to feel protective of her.

"They adapt," I said.

"Well how silly of them," Mother Nature giggled, putting her hand briefly on my shoulder.

"Still," Val continued, "it must, like, take *courage* to live up there."

She seemed proud of this word as well. I was studying her speaking habits so closely I couldn't think of anything sensible to say myself. "Well, courage is the better half of valor," I offered.

"*Val* is the better half of valor," Cody corrected, raising his eyebrows at me from over the top of his drink.

"No, actually it isn't very difficult in Wisconsin," I continued. "I suppose the greatest danger is dying from asphyxiation while warming up your car."

"Asphyxiation?" asked Robert.

"It's a cross between asparagus and the will to live," Christian explained.

"Could I, um, just, um, ask you one more quick question?" Val asked.

"*You couldn't ask a quick question if your life depended on it!*" Mother Nature screamed back at her. Almost everyone laughed, and Val good-naturedly joined in. But Cody wasn't laughing, he was looking at me. And I wasn't laughing, I was looking from Val to Cody back to Val.

"Sure," I said. "What?"

"Did you, um, like feel, um, closer to God in Wisconsin? I

mean, I always, you know, thought being so far north, you know, and the snow..."

Well, I'd given permission for the question, so it was my own fault.

I was saved by Mother Nature. "The way to a god's kingdom is through his stomach," she said, reaching for a chip and dip. "Besides, if you want to be closer to God, just talk to Reverend Flipping here."

"*Reverend* Flipping?" two or three of us asked at once.

Flipping reached in his wallet and picked out something looking like a business card. Sure enough, it said, "This is to certify the honorable REVEREND FLIPPING has been ordained as a minister in the CHURCH OF BOB."

"Church of *Bob*?" two or three of us asked at once.

"I think it's a parody of the Church of God."

"Do they parody the jokes as well?" I asked. "Like 'Bob is Bob spelled backwards'?"

"Needless to say, it isn't—"

"If it's needless to say, don't say it!" hissed Mother Nature, her gin and tonic poised threateningly over Flipping's head. Then she turned to me and asked, with the biggest, fakest smile I'd ever seen on a person not hosting a TV game show or asking for money, "Do you believe in God?"

"Of all your unanswerable questions," Cody intervened, "that is the most unanswerable."

"Why do you want to know?" I asked.

Her smile contracted like a muscle with tetanus. "I don't," she said. "I wasn't even curious."

There was a slight pause, during which Val and Robert took their leave.

"You should have seen them at my last party," Mother Nature began.

"We did see them," Christian reminded her. "We were there."

Mother Nature looked at them blankly, then became animated. "Now I remember! You were the mystery place!"

"The what?" I asked.

"I'll explain," Christian volunteered. "See, Mother Nature gave this party where everyone was supposed to come as a place. Several people dressed up like a Turkey, this really small guy came as Little Rock, this girl named Martha had grapes hanging all over her — Martha's Vineyard. You get the idea. Well, Flipping, Cody, and I arrived together, but we weren't wearing a costume. All night long people were complaining that we copped out, but we kept telling them that we really had come as a place. And they'd say, 'Yeah, Normal, Illinois, right?' And we'd say, 'wrong.' So finally, at the end of the night, we announced that we were going to tell everybody what place we were."

"Hey, let's do it for him," Cody interrupted.

"Okay, together . . ."

And they all three went into this routine — "We don't smoke Kent, we don't drink Bud, Norfolk, Norfolk, Norfolk, Virginia!"

Mother Nature left us with a toast, "A pox on your chickens!" but I was laughing almost too hard to hear her. Cody and Christian excused themselves for another drink.

"Do you live at home?" Flipping asked. I thought it was a strange question to ask someone in high school, but it turned out Flipping and Christian were living together in a garage apartment, finishing up school, working part-time jobs, and trying to get their band off the ground. It became apparent Cody visited them often, since they could do the sort of things at their apartment that couldn't be done at their folks' homes.

I suddenly remembered someone named Sarah, looked around but didn't see her. After a few inquiries, I learned she had gone to bed — alone — as it were, and locked the door. That a party was going on in her house was apparently nothing she felt compelled to think about any more.

It occurred to me that I should be in bed myself. Unlike these other people, who could probably sleep in late the next morning (a Saturday), I had promised my mother I would get up early and go with her into the country to gather firewood. I had argued that early September gave us plenty of time to gather wood before winter set in, but Mom was used to Wisconsin and Nebraska autumns and had her mind set on gathering firewood first thing Saturday morning. She had talked me into it by suggesting we grab a hot breakfast on the road, something I have always loved to do.

But now it was not so easy to leave the party, for I was enjoying the talk with Cody and his friends. When I announced my intention of leaving, they made things doubly difficult by inviting me over to "the Loft," as Christian and Flipping called their upstairs living quarters.

"We'll probably sit around over there for a couple more hours at least," Cody said, looking me in the eye in some earnest way that almost made me melt. "You're welcome to come." And somehow I knew this was an understatement, that not only was I welcome to come, but Cody seriously hoped I would. It was a tough decision, but I explained why I needed to get home, asked if I could take a rain check (immediately regretting the use of such a weatherworn expression), then made my exit.

At home in bed I had the first in a series of unusual dreams starring Cody. This first night I attributed it to alcohol, although I had not drunk much at the party. But other nights followed in which I could find nothing to blame my dreams on except my over-active subconscious, and Cody's hold on my thoughts. Often I would lie awake with insomnia, then awaken from some incredible dream after only an hour or two of sleep.

The first dream was short and relatively simple compared to some that came later. It went like this:

I was at school, in the locker room after gym class, getting dressed. The other boys must have left already, for I was alone. Usually I was one of the first to shower and get out of that place, but this was a dream and in the dream being alone in the locker room didn't seem at all unusual. Then I realized I wasn't alone, for Cody was standing in the entrance leading to the showers, his hands gripping an overhead railing, while his nude, muscular body assumed various seductive, although quite natural, poses. I looked at him hesitantly, saw he was staring at me, apparently waiting for something. Then I looked away from him, back at my clothes on the bench. I could feel him walking toward me, though I didn't look up. He made a slow approach, then, when he was upon me, about a foot away, something amazing happened. He was suddenly all over me and even through me, having assumed some spectral, vaporous quality — I could feel him passing through every cell of my body, taking charge in a way, just visiting in a way. I could also hear his thoughts, for they were becoming my own.

"I remember friends like brothers, when friends were what we lived for. I remember friends always there, to live your life with. Then it was you and me 'cause we were in this crazy wreck together, that being what we had."

And something within me awakened and replied, *"It was everything."*

Then I awoke in a sweat. There was something about the dream I could not escape, even awake. It was the feeling of the dream, which I could still sense cruising through the cells of my body, some clicking, static, electric buzz which refused to leave.

I got out of bed and walked down the hall to Freddy's room, but Freddy was asleep, as I knew he would be. I went into the kitchen and drank a glass of orange juice. Then I returned to my room, got back in bed, but did not go to sleep.

Three

The first thing I noticed on entering my history class Monday morning was Cody's having switched seats to the desk directly behind my own. More curious was his being present at all, since Cody was usually one of the last students to enter the classroom. Walking to my desk, I took off the sweater I was wearing, draped it over the back of my chair, then said hello. Normally I would have said hello first, but Cody, involved in writing something, had not even looked up at me. When I did say hello, a few seconds passed before he ripped out some pages from his loose-leaf notebook and held them out to me.

"Good morning, Trotsky," he said, smiling broadly. "Read this when you get the chance."

Well, I read it all right, without waiting to be given the chance, for the first sentence was all it took to grab my attention — "I was standing in the locker room, watching him, unobserved." Of course I had to keep reading, not even trying to hide it from Mrs. Kraemer. I had no idea what she was doing with the class that hour, but I did know she would not interrupt my reading. I felt protected, somehow.

What I read in Cody's story ran a distant parallel to my dream of early Saturday morning, with everything turned around, as it would have been from his perspective. The main character was watching someone dress in the locker room and felt himself being drawn to this person as if by a magnet. Suddenly realizing what he must do, he attacked the person, not physically, but spiritually, making them one unit. In the story, Cody called it "bodhisattva," which is to say they were each the other's bodhisattva and together they also formed a bodhisattva. This part of the story, I must admit, left me foggy, but I was already in a daze, knowing I had just read something impossible: an account, by someone I had dreamt about, of *my* dream! *Déjà vu* always fascinated me, but this new phenomenon I found almost too strange to appreciate.

I read the story again, running his words through my mind over and over, but none of the words seemed to be real or to make any sense. It was like when you write a word, a simple word you've written all your life, which for some reason doesn't look spelled right, and doesn't seem to mean anything.

After class, I returned the story to Cody with a comment to the effect that it was pretty bizarre. He looked at me questioningly, then nodded his head slowly and started to walk away. "Somehow I thought you knew," he said over his shoulder. I stood frozen in my tennis shoes until he was well out of sight.

Naturally, I thought of nothing else all day.

In gym that afternoon I was dressed and on the bleachers by the time Cody made it to the locker room. My stomach in knots, I wondered if I could get through class without having to excuse myself. Cody came out of the locker room looking around for me, I suppose, as he stopped looking around once he spotted me, nodded a distant greeting, then joined some friends on the gym floor until the coach called everyone over to the bleachers for roll. Not looking at Cody much for the rest of the hour, I didn't know if he was looking at me or not.

I thought about skipping my shower after class, but sniffing my underarm, thought better of it. As I came out of the shower room, I passed Cody going in. When our eyes met just for a moment, I was annoyed to see him looking almost as if he were laughing at me. I dressed quickly, though not quick enough to miss seeing Cody again. While I almost expected him to stop in the entrance of the shower room, assuming some pose as he did in my dream, he merely walked over to sit down beside me, his locker being just across from mine.

"It's not raining today," he said. "How about getting together later tonight?"

I had to think a minute before realizing what he was talking about, then remembered my cliché at the party about taking a rain check.

"I have a job interview," I said. "Maybe some other time."

"Doesn't last all night does it?" he persisted. "I have to work myself until eight or nine. I was thinking maybe after that."

"I've got some things to do tonight," I lied. "But thanks for asking me."

"Some other time then," he said, sounding fairly hurt, then turning his attention to getting dressed. When he spoke again it was to someone he knew further down the bench. I looked at him hard for just a moment, as he was pulling his shirt on over his head, suddenly realizing that this was the amazingly attractive boy I had been in a panic to know. So what the hell was I doing making excuses not to see him?

The bit about the job interview was a lie. True, Sarah had arranged an interview for me with the phone company, but when my mother heard about it she had savaged the idea, insisting no son of hers would work for that goddamned corporate scuzbag (her description). She then tore into me about why I needed a job in the first place, offering, when I told her I didn't have money enough to buy all the music I was craving, to increase my allowance. I argued that I was too old to be kept on allowance, so she simply repeated herself, this time calling it a stipend. The reason for this generosity was her fear of my grades falling off if I got an after-school job. It was not actually the value of grades as a measure she cared about, but her wish that I attend a good college for which the grades would be important. Although she had graduated from Wisconsin and Nebraska, and my father from the University of Chicago, I think she had Columbia in mind for me. In any case, I hesitated at her offer to give me more money. She had a good job teaching at the university but it wasn't *that* good, and her abundant generosity had landed her in trouble before, more than once. Still, agreeing I couldn't work for the Bell system in good faith, I had called Miss Whistle to cancel the interview.

Home from school, I thought some more about my behavior with Cody, understanding my actions less each time I reconsidered them. I played Freddy a game of cards after dinner, then said I was going out for a quick ride and started for the door.

"Ride where?" Freddy asked. "Why doncha ask me to go?"

"Not this time, okay?" I said.

Freddy and Mom just looked at each other in puzzlement. While I could have claimed I was going to the library or something, it had never been my habit to tell them lies. They appreciated this and didn't question me any further about my destination.

Cody was there, perched atop his desk, sipping at a soft drink and reading a novel by Hermann Hesse, who just happened to be my favorite author. I was pleased we would have something to discuss besides ourselves and school.

"Would you like a drink?" Cody asked, in reply to my hello. I sampled his beverage, then stepped outside and bought one for myself — not wanting it so much to drink as to hold, reacting to the same impulse which makes one wish for a cigarette at times, even if one doesn't smoke.

We sat, practically motionless. Our arms moved every few seconds, lifting soft drinks to our mouths ... and our hair moved, too, as the wind gushed about, around and through the station, a pleasing prelude to more rain. Cody continued to read, expressionless, as if he were trying to emulate Siddhartha, although the novel in his hand was actually *Beneath the Wheel*. Then he put the book away, hopped gracefully down from atop the desk, and walked casually out to the gas islands. He had a customer. I watched him service this customer, a good-looking man in his late twenties or early thirties. They were talking in a friendly manner and Cody was laughing at things the guy said. I felt a darkness spread over me like the shadow of an eagle's wing over a field mouse. It was a darkness which at first I could not identify — something new, something alarming and terrible.

Cody came back in the station to get change from the register. As he passed me he formed his hand into the shape of a pistol, pointed the loaded index finger in my direction and mouthed the word, "Bang!"

Then he lingered with the man for what seemed too long a time. Once back inside, he seemed to waver between returning to his book or paying me some attention.

"I've finished up early with my chores," I told him. "You still interested in getting together later?"

Cody seemed to sigh inwardly, nothing audible. "Actually, I've made other plans, since I thought you were occupied."

I could feel my heart sinking deep into my gut. "Guess I missed my chance," I said, hoping for a smile. He gave me a questioning look instead.

"Maybe I was wrong about you," he said.

As the combination of silence and his stare began to make me uncomfortable, I asked, "What do you mean?"

Cody withdrew into thought, his face gradually tightening into something of a frown. But even when frowning he exuded a warmth, perhaps even with greater intensity, a fiercer fire burning.

"I've been arguing with myself all evening about whether or not to come up here," I said.

Cody smiled. "The problem in arguing with yourself is you can never win more than you lose."

I returned the smile, thinking of the converse statement, which I chose to leave unstated. Instead, I took a deep breath, then began my apology. "I'm sorry I couldn't—"

He waved me silent with his hand.

"No, it doesn't matter," he said finally. "But I've got a busy week ahead, so why don't we try to get together this weekend? Is Friday night okay with you?"

"Yes," I agreed. "Friday's good."

Looking straight at me, hardly even blinking, Cody smiled again. "I like you, Trotsky," he said, with such ease and simplicity as to seem the most natural thing anyone could ever say to me. But it wasn't something I was used to hearing. Trying not to appear as dizzy as I felt, I smiled back at him. Rather than returning the compliment, I said, "Yeah, I thought you did."

Then Cody did the damnedest thing. He jumped off the desk straight on top of me, stunning me almost as much as in the dream when he'd jumped into me, and sending us falling over backward in a folding chair. I don't expect he meant this to happen, for he had to act quickly to halt our fall and protect my head from the concrete floor. I think we were both too startled to speak.

"Cody!" a voice from behind us barked. Cody immediately turned scarlet. "What kind of behavior is this, may I ask?"

Recovering quickly, Cody replied, "I guess you can, you're the boss," while his face continued to flash crimson. I went through a repertoire of expressions myself, ultimately freezing on agony. The gentleman, who really *was* Cody's boss (a Mr. Vandaway, according to his work jacket), looked rather disheveled himself, a look made all the more pronounced by the way his mouth kept opening and closing like a fish yanked ashore. I don't think he knew what to make of the scene he had just witnessed. In any case, he chose to focus on the mundane rather than the conspicuous.

"Try to treat my chairs a bit more kindly, son," he said, bullfrogs leaping from his throat with every syllable.

"Yes sir," Cody replied.

Mr. Vandaway looked helplessly around the station, perhaps, subconsciously, for more overturned chairs or other signs of furniture abuse.

"Well, I just dropped in to bring you these oil funnels. Somebody must have taken the other one this morning. I forgot to mention it when you came in, but I guess you noticed it wasn't here."

"Yes. I looked for it. Found it in the restroom.'

"Now how do you suppose it got in there?" Mr. Vandaway asked testily. I figured he had probably left it there himself, all the more reason for his testiness. Mr. Vandaway, well on his way toward old age, hated all the symptoms, to be sure.

Cody just shrugged as Mr. Vandaway helped himself to a wad of money from the register. Once he had left, Cody whistled softly that type of whistle meaning "close call," then, giving me a charming, timid grin, said, "Sorry if that embarrassed you."

"I'm sure it embarrassed you more."

"But I'm the one . . . oh, what the hell, it's over. So how has your day been otherwise?"

"You've been the major part of it."

Cody nodded, as if he knew that but had just forgotten it momentarily.

"Tell you what," he said. "You give me some time. I don't know exactly what we're dealing with, but I know there's something between us, maybe something as old as the earth. I had a dream about you Friday night after that party. It was the strangest dream I've ever had. Somehow I felt like you had the same dream, I think maybe even at the same time, 'cause when I left the party I went straight home, not over to the Loft like I'd planned. Anyway, I wrote that story about my dream."

"You were right," I told him. "I had the same dream, except it was from the opposite viewpoint — I was the one getting dressed in the locker room, and then it was like I'd been invaded by you. Even after I woke up I felt something going through me like a kind of buzz. I could almost hear it."

"So could I."

Once again, all we could do was stare at each other. It was time to take my leave, I felt, for we had said enough for one night.

"Well," I began, getting up from the chair. "I'll see you 'round at school, and . . . Friday."

Cody gave me his killer grin and said, "Thanks for stopping by."

When I arrived home, Freddy was watching a National Geographic special on the television and my mother was taking a bath. I sat down to watch the special and soon Mom came out with a bag of body oils and facial creams, joining us in watching the show while she made herself soft. I liked my family, and I almost felt like telling them so. Of course, Mom probably would have taken my temperature at such an announcement, so I just tried to watch the special without looking too distracted — not an easy task, even though the show was a good one about penguins.

Often when I went to bed, as soon as I turned off the light and crawled under the cover, my mind would go "Showtime!" and commence a private screening of short subjects from my past: of a girl who tried to coax me into sex when I was barely thirteen, of a drivers' education instructor who would crack me up with wry comments about the way people drove, of another girl in Lincoln with whom I went swimming until she got in the habit of grabbing me by the nipples and squeezing until they turned blue. Tonight was a film-festival, or perhaps only previews of subjects to be covered during REM sleep, if I ever made it that far. I thought about the store clerk at Padre Island last summer. Apparently English, she'd replied, "Oh, don't be daft! Of course we do," when I'd asked if they had tanning oil. Although I had been waiting all my life for someone to tell me not to be daft, I'd expected to hear it in England someday, from one of Mom's relatives, not on the Texas coast from a convenience store clerk.

Next, I thought about the time Mom bought Freddy and me walkie-talkies one summer, failing to mention she'd also bought one for herself. So, one day Freddy and I were out planning an ambush on a girls' swimming party down the street, discussing back and forth on our walkie-talkies how we could come up on both sides of the yard and hurl dirt clods into the pool, when suddenly Mom blurts out over the air, "Trotsky! You and Freddy get home this minute!" Talk about a fright...

And then I'm remembering when, just before we moved from Wisconsin, Mom took us for a ride around some of the neighborhoods we'd lived in. We drove by the house where the boy had been forever overhauling his cars, always up on jacks in the front yard, where they didn't belong. And the house next to it with the "Day Sleeper" sign on the door, a rare species, the people I'd never seen, not once in three years, only heard rumors about. Some guy had said they were thieves, that he'd seen them carrying five televisions into the house one night. I made countless attempts to spy through their windows, but the curtains were always drawn.

There was the house with all the kids running around half-dressed, cute kids with no money, nothing to do but grow up mean, but not really if you got to know them. I remember how Kevin, the oldest, had maintained a distant respect for me, being older still, and had come around one morning to shyly ask if we were really moving. Disappointment turned to joy when, remembering the fort I'd built in some nearby woods, he'd asked if he could have it, and I'd told him he could. Together we'd gone to the fort and carved his name in the wooden door, just below my own, which he promised never to remove.

There was the jungle house where the dizzy girl with the dizzier mother lived with plants all over the place, no room to sit or stand, no TV, just plants.

And the house that was a little bit better than the other houses, with the sisters who were a little bit prettier than the other girls, with the trampoline in the yard each summer, and everyone jumping up and down up and down up and down and sometimes bounding off into the street in front of cars, almost getting killed, but I always knew she wouldn't stay, the one my age, or any of them, 'cause the neighborhood wasn't attractive enough for their money, not really. But it was we who had moved instead.

I remember Mom pointing out the bridge where I'd missed the frog and broken my nose. Unconscious, waking up in a hospital, the first time I'd been in one since my birth, and sure enough they served me Jello, and we had to pay extra for the TV. I heard all about how Mom had broken all kinds of traffic laws trying to get me to the hospital, until a policeman stopped her, but then seeing the situation, had provided a sirened escort. After waking up in the hospital, and hearing this story, I'd asked, "Is my bike all right?" which made everyone laugh, claiming it was just like me to ask that. I wondered what some-one else might have asked, but nothing came to mind.

I was having no luck at all falling asleep. I could feel my eyes sending messages: they were tired and would like to close for the season. Although I did get some sleep eventually, it was exceedingly light, and around five in the morning my eyes flew open with such vigor that I knew trying to go back to sleep would be hopeless. So I lay in bed, watching as more and more sunlight poured through the curtains. Finally, I got up to use the toilet, and on my way back down the hall I looked in on Freddy. He was sleeping blissfully as usual, and even seemed to be experiencing a pleasant dream. I wondered who was in it.

Back in my room I slipped on a pair of jeans and sat on the edge of my bed, toes playing with the curls of the carpet. A remarkable sensation of perception quite suddenly dawned in me, as if balls of cotton had been removed from my ears. I began listening to the birds singing outside — wanting to under-stand them, wondering if they could understand themselves. What might your average bird be thinking on a morning like this? Their music was beautiful, so I began to supply whatever lyrics I chose. One could make them say the damnedest things.

When I was a child, I liked to pretend all the trees and shrubs in our yard were hotels. In a sense they were, for I was constantly aware of the various birds and squirrels checking in and out, although I don't recall being aware of this metaphor at the time. Perhaps I invented this fiction because it was more fun, when trimming hedges, to think I was remodeling a luxury hotel. However, as I don't recall thinking of this at the time either, I believe it must have been sufficiently amusing just to think of the trees and shrubs as hotels, no further explanation necessary. Now, listening to the birds, I began to analyze my gradually acquired wont of making things complicated, hoping I could reverse the process.

I began to hear other things, too, not just the birds. I could hear a medium-size Southern city awakening, with cars, factories and construction sites merging to form an urban, industrial symphony.

I don't know how long Mom had been standing in my doorway watching me. She was in her robe, wearing no make-up, though she had brushed through her hair when she got out of bed. It was exactly the way I liked most to see her, for I felt she was never more beautiful, never more herself. I could tell she wanted to ask me what was on my mind, but didn't want to seem nosy. She knew I suffered with insomnia (she always told me I inherited it from my father), and she knew I suffered most when something was bothering me or when I was dying from anxiety attacks. She asked if I would like a cup of coffee. I told her I would like that very much. Then the sound of her knocking about the kitchen blended with this other symphony I was hearing, and soon I could also hear the twenty-four-hour news channel from the portable black-and-white she kept on the kitchen counter. Our house seemed to be full of little machines that made noises. Having already put on my jeans, I went to my closet and pulled out the most anonymous-looking shirt I could find to wear to school.

For the rest of the week I took exceptionally good care of myself, fearfully hoping to be feeling and looking good on Friday. In a very literal sense, I was too sensitive. Things in the air not only caused my nose to run, my skin to crack, and my eyes to itch, but at times made me moody, nervous, and angry. My sense of "presence" was sensitized to the point where every little thing kept me awake — I couldn't block out noises the way others do. Nor could I easily assimilate hurt feelings or remain unaffected by the injustices in the world. It was a complex, sweeping case of being too aware, too sensitive.

Thursday, my eyes were bloodshot from pollen and lack of

sleep. I thought of calling Cody and canceling our plans, as if I were a businessman flying off to Houston unexpectedly. But I wanted desperately to see him. Sure, I had seen him every day at school, but we didn't speak or even look at each other much except to nod a quick hello. It wasn't any good with all those others around. I knew whatever it was we had to say should wait until Friday, when we could be by ourselves. I knew Cody felt the same.

By gym on Friday, we still hadn't made plans on how to get together after school. Cody was sitting beside me, facing his locker across the bench. I liked this arrangement because we didn't have to look at each other dressing and undressing. There was something unfair about these daily opportunities to see each other nude. Although it was his looks which first attracted me, I would as soon have waited until I knew Cody better before knowing them so thoroughly. His face was intimidating enough as it was. Still, I had caught enough glimpses of Cody in the locker room and showers to know his body was equally engaging. He was strikingly well-toned, with sleek, hairless skin stretched tight across his frame, hard and tender, the embodiment of austere economy. I felt anyone would have wanted him.

While we were dressing, I asked Cody if he had to work that evening.

"No, I don't work tonight," he answered. "But I do have some things I need to do after school. If you'll give me your number I'll call you 'round seven, if that fits in with your plans."

"Yes, that's fine."

I gave him the number, then he asked if there was anything special I wanted to do. I said there wasn't.

"Well, I can show you the Loft and we can hang out with Christian and Flipping for a while. But before we do that I'd like to go somewhere and get plastered while we get to know each other better."

"That sounds great, but where could we get a drink around here?"

"I know a place that'll serve us. My older sister's husband owns it and usually bartends himself. As long as we're discreet and sit in a dark corner we'll be okay."

"Sounds great," I repeated.

I had noticed several of Cody's friends, or maybe just acquaintances, listening in on the conversation. It was obvious from the looks we were getting that a lot of other guys wouldn't have minded meeting Cody for a drink. There was something about him which made you feel good, made you feel alive, just being with him.

At exactly seven p.m., Cody phoned, asking me to meet him in an hour at a North Little Rock club. After hanging up, I decided I was too restless to sit around the house until it was time to leave, so I drove my car to the outskirts of the city, where the Interstate 430 bridge crosses the Arkansas River. Away from the lights, you could see a few stars, and a brilliant harvest moon was like blood on the water. To the west, Scorpio was falling into the Ouachita Mountains.

I was back in civilization much too soon. With time to kill, I drove through the backstreets of North Little Rock, a city made up mostly of backstreets. Called "Dog Town" by some residents in Little Rock proper, North Little Rock was poorer, more conservative, and more religious than its big sister across the river. I noticed the billboards — a campaign ad for "the sheriff that shoots straight," only someone had added an "s" to the last word, creating a humor I wouldn't have expected to find in Dog Town. Another billboard — "Future home of Assembly of God Abundant Life Chapel." I wondered why the prankster hadn't changed this one to "Future home of Assembly of God Abundant DEATH Chapel." Perhaps because, like Jonestown, Guyana, it was more difficult to reach. Next to this future home was a day-care center with one of those ugly portable signs in the front yard, the kind of sign with black letters the kids are always changing around, only in this case they didn't need to, since the sign read: "Openings in infants and toddlers." A hell of a way to put it.

As I turned the next corner, I heard something which sounded very much like a gunshot. I hoped it was a car backfiring, or a firecracker, but it sounded more like a gun. Then I heard it again, louder, closer than before. Living in America was exciting, for always in the back of your head was the knowledge that at any given moment someone might shoot you for no reason whatsoever.

I beat a fast path to the address Cody had given me, arriving by ten minutes of eight. I was astonished to discover a club named the Magic Theatre. One thing we hadn't discussed was whether to meet inside or outside. I figured Cody wasn't there yet, and since I didn't relish the idea of walking in and having to explain, to whomever might intercept me, what I was doing there, I decided to wait in my car for at least fifteen minutes.

The time passed slowly. I was anxious and fidgety. Wishing for the trillionth time that I had a cassette player in my car, I did the best I could with the radio dial. The music didn't help much, just set my nervousness to a trivial beat. I suppose eight minutes must have passed before a white car pulled up at the curb across the street, dropping off Cody. The car sped away too fast for me to tell if the young woman driving was anyone I'd seen before.

Cody waited for several cars to pass, then crossed the street, looking better than ever. As he walked through the parking lot, I watched him closely, noticing the intensity of his eyes as they searched among the cars, looking for me. His expression upon seeing me changed immediately to boyish pleasure, which made me feel guilty for not having hailed him first.

"Have you been here long?"

"No, not long."

On the door of the club were the words, "For Madmen Only."

"Did you name this place?" I asked.

Cody grinned and opened the door. We walked inside, where Cody introduced me to his brother-in-law, Jim, then asked if we could find a dark corner and have a few beers. Jim, clad in a Razorback sweatshirt, looked me up and down and said, "Hell, Cody, he's even smaller'n you, and ain't no way you'd pass for twenty-one. Why couldn't you be tall like your brother?"

"I'm tall enough," replied Cody. "Besides, I'm still growing. I may break six feet yet."

Jim just stared at him. "Hell, kid, the only way you'll ever break six feet is if you hit 'em with a brick!" And he walked away, laughing at his joke. "Go in yonder to the back room and grab that table by the kitchen door. I'll bring along a pitcher in a minute."

"Thanks, Jim," Cody said. Putting a hand on my shoulder, he led me to the back of the club. On the way, I noticed the doors to the johns were labeled "pointers" and "setters."

"Cute," I said.

"Not very," said Cody. "They used to be labeled 'Elton' and 'Olivia Newton,' but then Elton John announced he was bisexual and all the boys got confused."

I glanced at him over my shoulder, he smiled back at me, we found our table.

"Do they serve food here?"

"Just nachos and burgers. Are you hungry?"

"No. Just wondered what the kitchen was for."

Jim arrived with our beer. "You boys enjoy yourselves, but if any cops come in tonight, you hightail it in that kitchen and start washing dishes like you work here!"

Cody saluted, and Jim left us to ourselves.

We cruised our way through two pitchers of beer quicker than I thought possible. Although not much of a drinker, I was nervous and would have consumed anything on the table just to have something to do. Conversation ran smoothly, reaching with each succeeding mug of beer farther and farther into the bohemian hinterland.

"How'd you like *Beneath the Wheel*," I asked.

"Remind me next time we're in gym, I'll show you the tread marks on my back."

"Got to you, huh?"

"Devastating."

During this exchange it dawned on me that Cody had been staring into my eyes for quite some time. I had never experienced this before, could not recall anyone ever looking at me for so long. It was hypnotic, for I could not look away. Cody, finally, broke the eye contact, smiling sweetly to himself, nodding his head in affirmation, whispering, "all right," softly, for the angels to hear.

We discussed music, Nostradamus, politics, and the golden mean. Cody seemed to relish off-beat topics of conversation as much as I did, so it was with great enthusiasm that we discussed cicadas, those obstreperous insects who spend thirteen or seventeen years underground, ultimately emerging in spring to sing, mate, lay eggs, and die within a month. Cody was excited because the thirteen-year brood in Little Rock was scheduled to emerge the following spring. In Wisconsin and Nebraska, the cicadas had belonged to the seventeen-year broods. I had witnessed an emergence quite some time ago, remembering it vividly.

Cody told me what little he knew about the Masons. His grandfather had been a Mason, and Cody remained solemnly intrigued by the memory of ritualistic ceremonies performed at his grandfather's funeral.

From the Masons, Cody jumped to Tibetan medicine. I learned about Tibetan monks believing a child is born into the world with a "burden of sin," carried over from previous lives. After birth, the child either repels demons or draws them to him, depending on the burden of sin. I asked Cody if he believed this. He just shrugged and told me they also believed having sexual intercourse with a pregnant woman was almost certain to give one cancer. I started to laugh, but Cody stopped me.

"How do you know it's not true?" he asked. "Just think, if it is true..."

He didn't finish the sentence, but began another:

"I do believe in karma. I don't think things 'just happen.'

Like us meeting, and those dreams we had — those things don't just happen, it's all cause-and-effect, probably from our past lives."

"Our past lives?" I interrupted.

Cody frowned. I got the feeling he hadn't expected me to be so skeptical. Well, I couldn't help it. Skepticism was my second nature.

"If you don't feel it already, I'm not sure I can explain it to you," Cody said softly, still frowning. "We're *old souls*, Trotsky. That's the only explanation. We've probably known each other in several past lives. Maybe we were friends, maybe we were lovers — all I know is, I feel the bond is very strong."

I'm not sure how I would have responded if I'd been sober. But then, I don't know if Cody would have said this if he had not been drinking. I was spacing out, contemplating a reply, when I noticed silver-badged, gun-toting culture shock mingling with the crowd in the other room. I grabbed Cody by the arm and we reached for the kitchen door, just as Jim flung it open, yanking us inside.

Instead of showing us the dirty dishes, Jim showed us a side exit to the parking lot and asked us to use it.

"Don't know why I risk my neck for you, Cody," he said, obviously in a bit of a panic. "Get out of here quick!"

"We haven't paid," Cody said, reaching for his wallet.

"Would you just get your ass gone!" he said and shut the door behind us.

Cody seemed sad as we walked to my car. "That's never happened before. I wonder why the cops would choose tonight to show up?"

As the question did not require me to answer, I remained silent. In my car, I found it hard to drive and talk at the same time, therefore Cody did most of the talking while I paid attention as best I could. Unfortunately, Cody was having a hard time talking and remembering to give directions, so I had to interrupt repeatedly, asking which way to go. Each time, he seemed to hesitate a little longer before answering.

Cody was talking about some of the girls he'd dated. I was wishing he had chosen another time, for I wanted to see his expressions as he talked. He said something about a girl into witchcraft, whom he had been with the night before. She had frightened him. There was a pause, then he asked if I was serious about Sarah.

Serious about Sarah? It was an interesting way to phrase it.

"I think we're friends," I said.

"Sarah's good fun."

"Christian seems to think she's frightening."

"Well, she *is* frightening, but in a fun sort of way. The girl I was with last night was just frightening, period."

As we walked up the stairs to the Loft I could see eerie, blue television light escaping through the venetian blinds. Christian and Flipping, like millions of Americans, were apparently making their nightly voyage to the bottom of the sea.

The Loft was an old servants' quarters turned into something of a garage apartment. Although the mansion to which it once belonged had long ago burned down, the Loft remained. As I discovered later, the 1890s structure was not only pre-twentieth century, it was pre-intelligence. The stairwell, for instance, had a light switch at the bottom, but not at the top, allowing access to passers by, but not to Flipping and Christian, who either had to leave it on all night, or go down to turn it off, then walk back up in the dark. There was a third option used more frequently — they unscrewed the bulb.

Then there was the problem with the door, which locked automatically each time it closed. This meant they had to carry a key with them at all times, otherwise they could lock themselves out of their own apartment just going to get the paper or check the mail.

At the top of the stairs, Cody knocked once on the door, which then swung open, not having been shut completely. I could see Christian and Flipping sitting on a couch, watching a television turned upside down. The inverted soccer game provided an intriguing study of gravity. Apparently what had just transpired in the game did not favor the home team, for the crowd was abuzz with displeasure.

The smoke and smell of marijuana filled the room. Although grass was not a current temptation for me, I was glad Christian and Flipping were on some altered consciousness similar to my own. Upon seeing me, they offered barely perceptible hellos, and very stoned grins.

"Looks as if you're having an exciting evening," said Cody, with a motion toward the TV. Flipping switched the channel with some remote control device by his side. We were treated to photographs of the U.S. Marines battling stacks of tires in the Mojave Desert.

"Man, this is nowhere," Flipping said, flicking the TV off. "Someone put on some music."

"You got anything to drink?" Cody asked.

"Nothing alcoholic," Christian said, walking into the kitchen. "You want the usual Seven-Up?"

"How 'bout an unusual Seven-Up," Cody answered, although we had already heard Christian uncap the bottle.

"You got it," Christian called. "You want anything, Trotsky?"

"No, thanks."

"Why don't you look through the stack of albums by the stereo and pick out something?"

"Sure," I answered, as the phone rang in the kitchen. Cody and Flipping began a conversation about something I couldn't hear as I looked through the albums. First in the stack was Bubble Puppy. I heard Christian hang up the phone.

"Bubble Puppy?" I said.

"Hey, I found God listening to Bubble Puppy," Christian replied, re-entering the room.

"I've warned him not to play that shit," Cody said. I decided what the hell, and put on the Bubble Puppy. Christian handed Cody his Seven-Up. It was orange.

"Very funny," Cody said. "Who was that, anyway?"

"Red," Christian answered, motioning to the beige phone.

"Red?" I asked, just to be saying something.

"Red Stanley."

"Do they come in assorted colors?"

"Stanley probably comes in technicolor."

I made the connection that Red Stanley was the Stanley in their band, whom they had insulted reflexively at Sarah's party. I hadn't considered that Stanley might be his last name instead of his first.

"Hey, you don't play drums, do you?" Christian asked. "Maybe you could replace Stanley."

"*Nobody* could *ever* replace Stanley," Flipping said, looking at Christian as if he had just committed blasphemy.

"You should have seen him this afternoon!" Christian exclaimed, his voice rising. "Worse than ever! He's still not fully recovered from his mono, but he insists on singing anyway, even though he's got this sort of gargle in his throat that sounds something like a toilet flushing. Sometimes I just want to tell that jerk to take his ketchup commercial to a famous writer!"

We were all silent, until finally Cody said, "Christian, are you feeling okay? What you just said doesn't make a lick of sense."

"Well, Stanley makes me want to bastardize the English language!"

He looked as if he meant it. Meanwhile Cody was pouring his orange Seven-Up down the kitchen sink.

"Wasting that product!" Christian snapped. "Just because of a little orange dye."

Cody came out of the kitchen holding his gut. "I drank too much beer. I feel like I need to have my pumach stumped."

"Pumach stumped?" Flipping repeated. "Is that when you ask your pumach a question and it doesn't know the answer?"

"I know what the title of your first album should be," I said, to either or both of them. "You should play an instrumental and call it 'Too Clever for Words.'"

"Not bad," Flipping said. "But we haven't even thought up

a name for the band yet. We were thinking about 'Red Dye Young,' but that sounds too punk. Also, I think Stanley's afraid it's really a suggestion directed toward him."

"It wouldn't be a bad one," Christian added.

"He wants to call us 'The German People,' but he won't tell us why."

"It seems like you and Christian could come up with something better."

"We thought about calling ourselves 'Have a Nice Day!'"

"You must be crazy," Cody said, seriously.

"No, no, just listen for a minute."

Cody leaned back against a pillow, staring at the ceiling.

"See, we're gonna get Happy Face t-shirts and Happy Face stickers. We'll have Happy Faces all over the stage, on our instruments, our amps, our foreheads, *everywhere!* Then we'll come out and do these really morbid and degrading songs!"

"Morbid and degrading?" Cody and I screamed at once.

"Yeah, we thought we could use all those sappy lyrics Stanley keeps writing and just sort of scream them into the mikes with our faces all contorted. Christian's gonna change his name to P.O.W. and I'm gonna be M.I.A."

"You *are* kidding?"

"Yes, but wouldn't it be a smile?"

"So to speak," Cody grinned.

So well had I been entertained since entering the Loft that I hadn't noticed much what the place looked like. One detail was hard to miss, however. Someone (I found out later it was Flipping), having an affection for dead butterflies, had collected them (even the mangled ones scraped from the grill of his car), stuck pins through their abdomens, and placed them haphazardly around the walls and ceilings. Perhaps this, together with the four blue floodlights in each corner of the main, rectangular room, was meant to create a tropical paradise atmosphere. To me, however, the dead butterflies were unsettling.

"You should have heard how Cody messed up in Spanish today!" Christian said suddenly.

"Shut up, Christian!" Cody warned, good-naturedly. Cody began to walk toward him, but Christian went around a chair and, as Cody tried to get to him, told us the story.

"He was doing a translation exercise and one of the lines was 'Gracias, mi amigo.' Now any fool knows that means 'Thank you, my friend,' but Cody had to go and take the gender of the noun into account, so he translated it, 'Thank you, my *boy* friend.' You should have heard the roar he got from the class!"

Cody blushed, while everyone laughed at his expense.

Presently, Christian and Flipping settled in for more smoke. Cody joined them for the first hit, but after seeing me refuse the pipe, he also left them to it. I was getting tired, and just like he was reading my mind, Cody quickly made some perfect excuse for us to go. Before I knew it, we were back in my car.

"I hate going home," he said. "Maybe I should just stay here."

I didn't know what the feeling was like, to hate going home. I thought about it a moment while waiting for Cody's decision on what he would do. When he didn't say anything one way or the other, I got another idea and nervously asked if he'd like to stay at my house. Although my mother wasn't used to me bringing friends in unexpectedly, I didn't think she would mind. Undoubtedly, she and Freddy were in bed by this hour, and I was the one with insomnia, so I couldn't imagine us disturbing them.

The second I asked the question, Cody looked at me. He didn't say anything, just looked at me with his soulful blue eyes, as the street lamp caught the side of his smooth face to form some lonesome silhouette. Even drunk and tired, Cody's eyes continued to capture me with each mutual contact. Although he did not repeat the long staring again, each eye contact was a reminder we had done that, and some bond had been established, or re-established if one followed Cody's theory, which would not be broken easily. He nodded yes, he would like to stay with me, then asked what I expected him to ask: "Are you sure it's okay?"

By now I was feeling it was not only okay, it was essential. Some excitement began building within me, having been there all night in one form or another — the excitement of making a new best friend, the best, the purest, feeling I've ever known.

Mom and Freddy were in bed, as I expected. Cody offered some compliments on our house, especially my mother's taste in decor and choice of colors. I had to agree with him. She bought hefty furniture which looked nice but was sturdy enough to service *you* instead of the other way around. Just about everything in the den, from carpet to paintings, was some shade of brown or beige, giving the room a soothing, livable quality I could appreciate. I watched as Cody walked around examining various paintings and books, then I asked if he wanted anything from the kitchen. He suggested coffee to stave off hangovers the next morning. I thought of my insomnia, but decided to hell with it, the coffee sounded good, a hangover did not. Unfortunately, I had never had reason to fool with the perculator, so we had to settle for instant.

Sitting at the kitchen table, sipping at the warmth, I began to question Cody about Christian and Flipping.

"Do you think they'll get anywhere with their band?"

"Yes, they're pretty good. You'll have to hear them play sometime. Flipping has a knack for coming up with good tunes, and Christian is a natural at singing — stage presence too, I bet, although they haven't been on stage yet."

"Who writes most of their songs?"

"Well, Stanley writes his own songs, and most of them really are bad. They need to get rid of him sooner or later. Christian and I write the other lyrics, my only contribution to this project."

"Why don't you learn to play something?"

"No talent. They tried to teach me bass, but I just couldn't pick it up."

"What are your lyrics like?"

"This is beginning to sound like a bad interview, Trotsky. Well, um, my lyrics are like self-indulgent a lot of the time, but I'm trying to get away from that. They're getting more political, but I'm not sure that's the direction I want to go, either."

"I'd like to see them."

"I'll show you some of my poetry sometime. It's a lot better than my lyrics."

I remembered then having read some of Cody's writing before.

"The story you gave me to read was good. I mean, aside from it involving me, it was very well written too."

"Thanks. I liked that one myself."

"You're a regular Renaissance man, you know. I mean, football, writing..."

Cody shrugged. "I guess so. I've always liked the idea of Buckminster Fuller's 'generalists,' but then, you're like that yourself."

Having never read Buckminster Fuller, I made a note to myself to do so. We finished our coffee, took turns making use of my toothbrush, then went to my bedroom. Cody immediately began sifting through my record and tape collection, just as I would have done in his place. He seemed pleased with what I had, and the few he commented on were among my favorites. Music has always been my main love in life, so it was gratifying to discover that Cody shared my tastes. I told Cody to pick out a tape and I'd play it at low volume. He chose a Joni Mitchell compilation I had put together myself.

"How long have you known Christian and Flipping?" I asked, trying to decide how loud I dared play the tape.

"We have a long history. I lived next door to Flipping for a long time. We went to elementary school together, then Flipping moved to another neighborhood and went to another junior high. That's where he met Christian, who had just moved here from Arizona — Tucson, I think. Christian introduced Flipping to drugs, and Flipping said, 'Pleased to meet you.' He and Christian were sort of the 'heads' at their school. I was going a straighter route myself, going out for sports, concentrating on my grades. I dunno, it probably had something to do with my favorite TV show as a child being 'The Match Game.' But then we ended up in the same high school, and I started doing the drugs with them because they were so much fun to be around. We each had our own reputation, but when we were together the only thing that mattered was having a good time. So we became best friends, although I got burnt out on the drugs pretty fast. I noticed you didn't smoke tonight either."

"No," I said, wondering how much of that chapter in my life I should tell him. "I did for a while when we lived in Nebraska. There wasn't anything else to do there. But my grades went straight to hell and I also noticed I was getting depressed all the time, thinking of suicide a lot 'cause I was just sick of everything. Then I sort of purposely OD'd one night when I was home with my little brother. Scared the hell out of him. Once they let me out of the hospital, I had to promise him I'd never do drugs again. So I promised, and I can't say I've kept it totally, but I've done a satisfactory job of it, I think."

Cody was sitting on the edge of my bed, crouched forward, hands pressed together. Through the hair hanging over his eyes, I could see him looking up at me, biting his lower lip.

"That's the most meaningful thing you've said to me yet," he said. "Maybe you'll be a good influence on me."

There was nothing I could say to that, so I went back to something he had said earlier:

"What kind of reputation did you guys have? You said something about all three of you having your reputations."

"Yeah, well, Flipping had hair down to his ass and was known by everyone as Mr. Drug Freak. I mean, that's when he got his nickname. Before the eighth grade he was Phillip Benning, then suddenly everyone was calling him Flipping. Christian's reputation was a little different. He knows just how much he can get away with, and he likes to take things to the limit. He and Sarah went to a school dance once with Sarah wearing a tux and Christian dressed in a wig and an evening gown. It was a Sadie Hawkins dance, so they just took things to the logical extreme. I thought maybe they'd gone too far that time, but everyone loved it."

Hesitantly, I asked, "Is Christian bisexual?"

"Not so much bisexual as gay," Cody said, without the slightest hint of embarrassment in his voice. "I've known that since the first day Flipping introduced me to him. I think everyone knows it, but you never hear people making jokes about him or anything like that. There are probably some jerks somewhere in the school who do, but I guess they're careful enough not to let me hear them, 'cause I never have."

I let this information sink in, deciding not to ask how he had known at once Christian was gay.

"Are he and Flipping lovers?"

Cody frowned. "I know Flipping likes the opposite sex, but he may be bisexual, I've never asked him . . . and I don't know exactly what his relationship is with Christian, although I've always thought they were probably just good friends the same way they're good friends with me."

Cody looked at me with an expression which seemed to say: Does that answer your question? We were both silent, perhaps because we realized there was nobody left to discuss except ourselves.

"You never told me what your reputation was," I said eventually.

"I've never really understood what it was, or what it is now, if you want to know the truth. When I was about nine or ten I was sort of small for my age and I hated to be picked on. I was an angry kid, and I went through a phase of giving people a friendly sock on the nose. Surprisingly, some people didn't appreciate the humor in that. But then I started growing, and I managed to outgrow my anger too. Now I think I confuse people. They can associate me with the weight-lifting team I was on for a couple of years, or they can associate me with the student council, which I was also on until I resigned last spring. Or they can associate me with challenging the teachers in class, or they can associate me with Flipping and Christian. It doesn't add up, not to most of them."

"I didn't know you were on the student council."

"You just met me, Trotsky. There are hundreds of things you don't know about me."

"I guess that's true."

"But at the same time I feel you know me pretty well. I think you knew me even before we said a word to one another — that's what's so crazy."

He was right, of course. That *was* the burning question.

"Did you understand what I meant in the story about being bodhisattvas?"

"No. I meant to ask about that."

"Well, you see, I've always felt religious, but I never could accept any religions I read about until I came across Buddhism through reading Hesse. I'm not a Buddhist, but I do admire a lot of their teachings. Anyway, back to the point — a bodhisattva is someone who attains enlightenment but doesn't enter into nirvana because of his compassion for others. He wants to stay behind and help them out. In all my reading, it was the bodhisattva who always impressed me the most, and I always felt that if I ever attained nirvana myself, assuming that's even possible, I wanted to have the courage to be unselfish and stay behind and help others."

"That's a very noble thought. I think my father must've felt the same way."

"You haven't told me what happened to your father," Cody said. And so I told him. Afterwards, he sat in silence for several minutes, just staring at the floor and saying, "Wow," very softly to himself.

"That's your karma, Trotsky! There's so much to you! And the great thing is you don't even seem to realize it. You don't seem to think you're anything special — but your humility *alone* makes you remarkable. I feel a sense of peace when I'm around you, and especially now that I'm in your house, in your room! I haven't even met your family yet, but I know I'm going to like them! And your father? Jesus Christ, Trotsky, what a legacy! No wonder when I had that dream, when I felt myself merge with your spirit, I suddenly felt like I could be a bodhisattva, and that especially together we could act as complements to each other and accomplish just about anything! Don't you feel that?"

Never had anyone said such things to me, or spoken with such authentic passion. Answering his question "yes" would border on a lie, I felt, for I could not duplicate his emotional level. Still, I was feeling something not unlike what he described: I needed Cody, or at the least I wanted him. He was looking for a complement, a bodhisattva, and I was searching for some seductive soulmate, a best friend. I gave him the "yes" he was waiting for. Perhaps there *would* be something spiritual about our friendship. Perhaps love was a chemical reaction to the spinning of the world.

"I hate to zap us back to reality, but I have to work tomorrow. Would you mind setting the alarm for me?"

"No problem," I said. "What time you need?"

"I have to be in at noon, and I'll need to go home first, so how about ten-thirty?"

Ten-thirty was only six hours away, so without a word we began to undress for bed. Even though we undressed in front of each other four days a week, I became hesitant and tried to take my time, letting Cody stay one step ahead. This wasn't hard since Cody went about it without hesitation, seemingly so much at ease we might have been at school. This lack of self-consciousness touched me, although I wasn't sure why.

I had a full-size bed in my room and there was never any pretense of someone sleeping on the couch or on the floor. Stripped to our underwear, we crawled under the covers.

When I turned off the reading lamp over the headboard, we were plunged into a darkness so complete all I could see for several minutes was the carousel of green LED lights flashing on the tape deck. Gradually those same lights illuminated the entire room, as my eyes adjusted to the change.

"Goodnight, Trotsky," Cody said, turning on his side to face away from me.

"Goodnight, Cody," I replied, with a mixture of disappointment and relief.

It seemed like no time before I could detect a change in Cody's breathing to the heavier, regular rhythm one associates with sleep. He must have been tired. I was tired. But I was awake, and lonely beside him. It occurred to me that to be lying in bed beside the person you love, and feel alone, was the most aching kind of loneliness, worse actually than being alone, although I wouldn't have wished Cody out of my bed for anything. Even when they made me miserable, I was thankful for my blessings.

I could now make out the shape of his face resting on the pillow, the arm across his chest, the top of a shoulder, a perfect nape, where I longed to place my lips, to feel his warmth, to taste his salt . . .

In the quasi-darkness the blond hairs on Cody's arm and the dark ones on my own looked silver. In the darkness we were not so different. A muscle here, an emotion there. The hair on your arms, the milk on my legs — penguins and piano keys, you and me.

Some natural clock awakened me at ten twenty-nine. This was a talent, or something, which worked for me more often than not, but wasn't reliable enough to trust completely, otherwise I'd have thrown the damn alarm clock out the window since the noise it made was like a barge on the Styx. When I awoke I saw that Cody had somehow managed to flop on top of me in his sleep. His weight lay upon me oppressively, and I wondered how I could have slept under him for however long we had been in that position. He wasn't lying completely on top of me, but one arm was flung across my chest and one leg crossed both of mine. His face was practically in my own and I could feel his warm breath on my neck. Carefully, I placed my only free arm across his shoulder, with my hand resting on his back. Cody stirred slightly, then was still. It felt so good I could only lay there, paralyzed by my own pleasure.

With the one hand I reached up to turn off the alarm, then lay perfectly still, feeling his breathing, synchronizing my own breath with his. Mentally I began trying to wake him up, and soon I could feel the muscles tense in his arms, then release their hold on me. Cody stretched himself awake as I pretended sleep, wondering about his reaction to beginning his day on top of me. I detected a pause, then felt him prying himself away. This provided a good excuse to yawn myself awake.

"Good morning," he said, glancing at the clock and immediately pushing himself from the bed. "I've got to hurry off, but you don't need to get up — go back to sleep."

Thinking it would be too weird for him to confront my family alone, without their knowing who he was, I got up anyway.

Mom was sitting in the living room, dividing her attention between a book and the news channel. I introduced her to Cody. She smiled and offered to cook breakfast. Cody told her it was a nice offer, but he had to get home fast, shower and change clothes, to be at work in an hour. Mom asked why he didn't just shower at our house, wear one of my shirts, and in the meantime — so he wouldn't have to go to work hungry — let her cook some bacon and eggs. Cody said something about not wanting us to go to so much trouble, but I put my hand on his shoulder and led him to the bathroom.

"Towels are under there. Shampoo's on the tub. Leave the door unlocked and I'll bring you some clothes."

Cody began to unbutton his shirt, shaking his head.

When he came out, my only thought was how much better my shirt looked on him than on me. Any of my shirts probably would have, since his shoulders filled them out better, but I ended up giving him that one anyhow, thinking I'd never be satisfied seeing it on myself again.

After breakfast, I drove Cody home so he could get his car and drive himself to work. When I let him off, I could think of nothing to say. Cody got out of the car, but stuck his head back in the door. "Hey, thanks," he said. And then he closed it.

Four

I had no further contact with Cody until I saw him in history class Monday morning, talking to a girl who had sat beside him before he switched desks. Now the girl had switched desks herself and was sitting by him again. I interrupted their conversation briefly to say good morning and see if they would include me in whatever they were talking about. As they were discussing going to a dance the night of the next football game, I sat down and left them to themselves. Cody asked me after class if I would meet him for lunch. We went to a relatively quiet place not far from the school, but off the beaten path. Christian and Flipping were with us, as they apparently met here — one of the few convenient places you could get good service during the noon hour — almost every day. Everyone had cheeseburgers except Flipping, who had a salad with no dressing. The vegetables, he said, should be allowed to express themselves without Robusto Italian intervention. Christian left early so he could cram for his next class. He was having a quiz in geometry, a class most students got out of the way during their sophomore year. Christian had put it off for two years because he hated math.

In gym, Cody was asked to be a team captain. His choosing me first again was met with puzzled amusement, since we were playing football, a sport in which my being relatively small was certainly no asset. Still, our team won easily, although my only notable contributions were some short catches when Cody, playing quarterback, got in trouble behind the lines.

As the week wore on, I grew bored waiting for something to happen with Cody, so I called Sarah again and made a date with her for Friday night. I liked to dance, and suggested going to the same event Cody was planning to attend. Sarah, however, had been out of high school for a year and felt she would be regressing if she went back for *any* reason, even to dance.

"I'll go back the day I can dance on Old Kindall's grave!" she said. Old Kindall was our principal. He wasn't really that old, it's just that his son had gone to the school at one time, and everyone had got in the habit of calling them Old Kindall and Young Kindall. Although the son had graduated some ten years ago, Old Kindall's name had stuck, primarily because, as Dickens might have said, it seemed unlikely he was ever young. Sarah hated him for once having told her to "stop dressing like a slut." Although Sarah's clothes were strange, they were in no way sleazy. She had never forgiven Old Kindall the remark, made in front of several schoolmates, including Christian, who had told me the story.

Since the movies were our logical choice for entertainment in Little Rock, and the features always changed on Fridays, Sarah and I decided we would wait until Friday to make our plans.

Cody and I had hardly exchanged a significant word all week. Each time I saw him he was engaged with someone else. Our night together began to seem like a dream. When I thought of him sprawled across me, it hardly seemed possible. Not when I watched him throw the winning pass to this real jerk-off in gym, nor when I saw him asking that girl to the dance. Not, in fact, at any time around other people, when he treated me as just another acquaintance. I wasn't treating him special, either, waiting instead to see what happened the next time I saw him alone. Every night I thought about going by the station, but somehow would get involved with Freddy playing one of those miniature hockey sets you can buy (we had started a league, like we did every year) and never make it. My car didn't need gas, anyway.

However, the week didn't pass without me having another strange dream. Only this time Cody wasn't in the dream at all and it had no pleasant aspect whatsoever. It was simply the most frightening nightmare of my life.

I had gone to bed thinking of how I wasn't living for much anymore. I was living for my mother and Freddy, and I was living to see what would happen with Cody ... but what else? Certainly not money, certainly not ambition, and last of all, decidedly not religion. Some demon in my subconscious decided to play upon this thought once I had passed into sleep.

I was lying on an immaculately clean bed, probably in the hospital, dying. Nobody had told me I was dying, but I could feel my death approaching. I could not open my eyes, but I could hear people crying near me from various parts of the room, clue enough I was near to death. More importantly, I didn't feel there was an ounce of life left in me, or even the will to live. I had accepted that death was a certainty, a fact waiting to take its course. I was not afraid, only wishing for the deeper rest. I could feel the life come unstuck and leave me, and then I was completely without thought. Minutes or days elapsed with my mind a complete blank until, with amazing vertigo, I began to experience an unwanted brainstorm. The first demand of my resurging brain was "What the hell happened?" Yet I remembered my death even before this question was completely formed, and my brain was demanding: If I'm dead and I'm still functioning *then what the hell's going to happen next and oh god did I live my life right? and how long is this darkness going to last?* I began to experience the fiercest terror of the unknown I have ever suffered. I thought for a minute I would have a heart attack from the fright, but again remembered I was dead already. And suddenly, I could feel myself moving. In no particular direction, seeing nothing but blackness, but moving just the same. I began to hear a distant, muffled noise. The sound of it struck terror in my soul, for I realized I was hearing the sounds of hell, or at least the wailing of the dead. Then I woke up, still in panic.

I was in my room, on my bed. I could hear the rain pounding hard against my window. Everything was right and proper, except my mind. I dared not fall asleep lest the dream once more grab hold and kill me. I feared it might have been a warning . . . from God or just some god, or from an unknown, heretofore dormant, part of myself. In any case, on this late September night upon my bed in Little Rock, I was afraid to sleep.

At length I grew tired of not sleeping, quietly made my way to the kitchen, had a glass of milk, read every word on the carton, then went to the bathroom. In the mirror I looked at myself with greater care than I had in some time, with this thought in mind: Why do I even exist? Will I live my entire life without feeling a sense of purpose? The face staring back at me showed little of this internal turmoil, hiding a troubled Trotsky from a world more accustomed to masks than true nature. A pleasant enough exterior, though in no way approaching the perfection of my friend, it concealed me the way a chassis might shield the inner workings of a car. Rarely did anyone trouble to look under the hood.

I remember looking at the clock at five-fifteen the next morning, still having gotten no sleep. I must have drifted off shortly afterward, for when the alarm went off at seven I was not capable of getting up to hit it. My mother sent Freddy in to perform this task, but I didn't even realize he was in the room until he started shaking me out of my stupor. When I finally was awake, I realized it was not a Chelsea morning. I almost fell asleep again while showering, and had to be talked into eating a breakfast which seemed too much trouble at the time. Freddy was eating some new cereal that featured an aggressively attractive boy on the box. Were advertisers, I wondered, going for pre-pubescent sex appeal? They probably were. I recalled someone in Lincoln I had known marginally who claimed he chose his breakfast cereal by which box had the cutest boy on the back. This guy had always annoyed me, and I had been doubly sure never to give him a hint of my sexual nature. He was the type of boy who, at age fifteen, had come out of the closet and run straight for the men's room. Everyone at school thought he was a joke — and I must admit, I did as well.

Despite my somnambular state, I went to school out of force of habit. People who hardly even knew me kept coming up throughout the day to ask if I was on drugs. I felt as bad as it is possible to feel, short of having a major disease.

Instead of calling Sarah again to discuss our plans, I decided simply to go by her office Friday afternoon as she was getting off work. She had a new sign on her desk, apparently home-made, which read: "Know ye that the Lord he is God. It is he tnat hath made us, and we are not elves."

Sarah, who had not seen me approach, fairly leapt when I asked what she'd done with her nameplate.

Recovering, she replied, "Oh, it's in this drawer here," and she kicked the bottom one of her desk. "I hate it when strange people call me by my name . . . except for you, of course." She then slipped a daring glance at my waist. "You're not looking for a job, are you?"

"Not that kind of job," I replied. "I just came by to see what we were doing tonight."

"You could have called."

I shrugged. "Yes, I could have."

Sarah looked at me, then at the clock, then grabbed her coat. "You want to follow me home? We can check the news-paper there and see what's going on."

Once we arrived at her house, I was introduced to her brother, whom I'd seen briefly the night of the party, then I had to endure meeting her parents. Sarah's mother, one of the daf-fiest creatures I've ever encountered, made a big deal of intro-ducing me to the dog. I was surprised that the resemblance be-tween Sarah, her brother, and the dog did not carry over to her parents. Mrs. Turner looked something like Queen Margrethe II of Denmark, and Mr. Turner, hairy and husky, resembled an ear of corn. He was a professor of zoology and widely regarded as Arkansas' leading expert on frogs.

After Sarah and I politely refused "din-din" five or six times, her mother joined the men of the family in either the den or the dining room, I wasn't sure which. Sarah and I found the *Arkansas Gazette* under a chair, chewed up slightly by Gee-Gee, the dog. Named by Mrs. Turner, Gee-Gee had been preceded by a smaller poodle called Fee-Fee. Sarah, her father and brother were holding their breath for Hee-Hee to come along.

"Aaagghhh!" Sarah screamed, frightening me, as I was on edge already from the encounter with her parents. "This ad for stationery has it spelled with an 'a'!"

I looked over her shoulder at the advertisement. "Maybe you can buy it but you can't take it out of the store," I suggested. Sarah jabbed me in the chest with her elbow.

Since nothing at the theaters looked particularly inviting, we decided we would try to get in one of the adult movie houses. Neither of us had ever seen a porno film. I wasn't convinced I wanted to see one then, either, but decided to go along since Sarah seemed excited about the idea. She went to change clothes, so I passed the time glancing through a burdensome dictionary that occupied the middle two-thirds of the coffee table directly in front of me. Turning to the section at the back titled "Common English Given Names," I looked up *Sarah* and found it on the page that began with *Salome*.

Sara, Sarah (Heb.) A princess.

Next I looked up Christian's name, knowing it would have something to do with that unfortunate but much-admired savior in whose name people had practiced heartening acts of benevolence or committed discreditable atrocities, depending.

Christian (L.) Dim. Christie.

Whatever that might mean. I tried without success to find *Cody*, didn't even bother looking for *Trotsky*, and finally decided to look up *Mike*, which was the name of Sarah's father and brother.

Michael, Mike (Heb.) Who is like God?

How should I know? I wasn't the blasted dictionary, after all.

Sarah returned, decked out in cedar-green jeans, a burgundy poncho, and hiking boots. Pleased she was feeling conservative, I asked, "Who is like God?"

Sarah stopped in her tracks, fixed me with a stare, and asked, "Do *you* know the answer, or am I supposed to tell you?"

I returned her stare.

"Is it someone I know?"

I returned her stare.

"Are they bigger than a breadbox?"

I nodded toward her brother. Sarah subvocalized the word *"Him?"* and dismissed the suggestion with an unpleasant grunt.

The doorbell rang. It was Christian. I called him a dim Christie, but he seemed happy to see us anyway. He inquired about our plans. We revealed them.

"Never work," was his only comment.

"Who is this guy?" Sarah asked. "First he implies we should actually have *plans,* and then he demands they be practical!"

Christian agreed to go with us, but as we made for the door, Sarah's who-is-like-God father asked where we were going. He had addressed the question to me, which was annoying, but since he had, I answered, "Oh, just driving."

He frowned. I added, "to the movies," and he accepted this answer with a nod, which was good enough for me. I never much cared for dealing with a parent not my own, and this paternal Turner was certainly no exception.

The movie house was obviously a grubby place showing cheap, amateurish flicks. The entrance was framed with an inordinate number of flashing lights, but even with our youth illuminated we had no trouble gaining entrance. Taking seats in the most vacant part of the theater, we entertained ourselves by making guesses as to what hole what character would next stick what object. Our speculation extended to include the man behind us as we pondered the meanings of the peculiar noises he was making.

When the movie was over, we left the theater, looked blankly at each other, then tried to decide what to do next. I suggested we find a place to eat, but Sarah claimed she wasn't hungry, and Christian assured us he wasn't Poland. I said I wasn't going to play, so they tripped me in the parking lot and stole the keys from my pocket. They ran to my car, got in, and sat laughing at me after locking all the doors. For nearly three minutes I stood shivering in the wind before giving in and saying, "I'm not Chile."

I climbed into the driver's seat, with Sarah beside me and Christian on the other side of the car. She put her arm around my shoulder and gave me a kiss. Her affection confused me until she suddenly spewed forth with some spur-of-the-moment poetry:

> You're not Body Beautiful
> with your disadvantaged asshole
> and your inverted navel
> But I like you anyway.

I pushed her away in protest, but she only laughed and flung herself up against me again, this time breathing heavily on my neck.

> When I first saw you
> with your Comic/Tragic faces
> you were drinking a carbonated beverage
> But I liked you anyway.

In spite of my decision to not be amused by anything she said, I laughed. Then I started the car and took off, still not knowing where I was taking us. On the radio a local newscaster was reporting on a press conference given by a "defective" Soviet swimmer. Before I could drive three blocks, Sarah yelled,

"Stop!" — slapping me on the stomach for emphasis. I stopped.

"What do they do in there?" she asked, looking across the street toward the Masonic Lodge.

Immediately I thought of Cody and the story he told regarding his grandfather's funeral.

"Have secret meetings," Christian volunteered.

"Can we get inside?"

"Somehow I doubt it."

"Do you want to try?"

Well, did I? Not especially, but I couldn't think of any reason why we shouldn't that was likely to convince Sarah or dissuade Christian, who was endorsing the idea with enthusiasm. I parked the car.

"Murder will out, as they say," I said, not entirely sure why I said it or what it meant.

"As *who* says?" Sarah demanded.

"People."

"Figures."

"Why does it figure?"

"Because it's a stupid thing to say, and people are stupid."

By this time we had reached the building.

"The door's not locked," Sarah said, pulling it open to prove the point.

"This is slightly scary," I said. It was. The building, in its stately architecture and cold marble columns and busts, was imposing. There were flags of all fifty states hanging from the walls in alphabetical order, although Maryland, always a flag to grab one's attention, had been stuck mysteriously between Georgia and Hawaii. It was deathly quiet.

Sarah and Christian had started up a flight of stairs toward a floor containing rows and rows of books. Catching up with them as they reached the top, I was already rehearsing what I would say if caught — "We, er, we were, um . . ." No, maybe I'd just let Sarah do the talking.

"Look at these strange books," she said to Christian. "The titles sound communist."

It was true, but not necessarily meaningful.

"Are you sure we should be in here?" I asked. It was a dumb, stupid, dumb question.

"I'm rather sure we shouldn't," Sarah answered.

Along the far corridor, Christian found a door nearly as imposing as the building itself, standing well over eight feet high, almost five feet wide, of dark wood embellished with brass. Christian looked at us, shrugged, placed his hand on the shiny knob and slowly turned it clockwise. To our collective amazement, it opened. Christian left it at a crack and we staggered ourselves vertically against it to peer inside. What we observed was strange indeed, evidently a type of ritual, surely not being conducted in English, the participants wearing elaborate robes and hats with tassels, not unlike those worn by the Shriners in parades. I was astonished at the solemnity with which they chanted.

With sudden alarm my eyes fell upon an old gentleman whose eyes had, with glaring alarm, fallen on me. He was rising. Only then did I realize Sarah and Christian had abandoned me and were waiting most impatiently at the head of the stairs. As I fled, the gentleman I had unwittingly alerted waddled through the door with an exclamatory wheeze, but we were leaping down the stairs just then, no longer able to suppress our laughter. To be running prestissimo through some stately building, fleeing a wheezing old man wearing a funny hat, seemed foolishly adolescent, but then we *were* adolescents, with inherent excuses for acting however foolishly we pleased.

Out of the lodge and back in my moving car, Sarah was in an exalted mood. The excitement of upsetting a Free and Accepted Mason apparently had made her day. I thought about Cody again, and what he would have thought of our adventure. I hoped he wouldn't hear about it, but didn't have the nerve to ask Christian not to mention it, therefore I was fairly sure Cody would hear the story from him. I was wrong, for Christian knew Cody better than I at the time, and certainly knew what was better left unsaid.

"So what do you think of Arkansas?" Christian asked, repeating a question I had heard often lately. Obsessed with their own image, Arkansawyers never asked what Nebraska or Wisconsin was like, only what I thought of Arkansas. What could one think of a beautiful, albeit conservative, Southern state which consistently sent one of the nation's brightest, most liberal Congressional delegations to Washington and repeatedly elected young liberals for state offices?

"I think of Arkansas as an independent culture," I told Christian. "If the United States was Europe, Louisiana would be France and Arkansas would be Albania. William Fulbright would have been Enver Hoxha, and Orville Faubus would have been King Zog." I could tell I was leaving them puzzled, which I felt was not only my safest course, but an appropriate example of how their state left me. "Right now I'm thinking I would like to live in a different state each year for the rest of my life. I'd like to go in a circle, hit Louisiana next, then Mississippi..."

"You're crazy," Christian told me.

"Alabama, Georgia, Florida, then up the East Coast..."

"Look where you'd be spending the best years of your life," Sarah warned.

"Then the states bordering on Canada."

"What about Alaska and Hawaii?"

"I'd take them after Washington, then circle in."

Christian was unconvinced. "Yeah, someday you'd find yourself sixty-five and living in Kansas."

I took Sarah home, where Christian got out to pick up his car. When I arrived at my own house, I noticed a man getting in his car and driving away. As far as I knew, my mother hadn't dated anyone in years, so a "gentleman caller" aroused my curiosity, and even my concern. Inside I found Mom sitting in a chair, looking as if she might cry at any minute.

"What's wrong?" I asked immediately. "Who was that man I saw driving away?" The first possibility to come to mind was Freddy's father, he being the only man I'd ever seen make her cry. But she said it was someone from the university, the chairman of the economics department.

"What'd he want?" I asked, wondering why he would be visiting so late on a Friday night.

"He wanted to warn me," she said. After allowing her plenty of time to continue, which she never did, I had to ask the obvious:

"Warn you about what?"

She got up, walked over to the television, turned it on, then snapped it off again. "Not to tell my students that I'm a socialist."

I stared at the back of her head as she stared at the vacant TV screen. He might, I thought, just as well have told her to keep it a secret that she was a woman.

"How can he restrict your freedom of speech like that?"

"I'm not sure that he can."

Actually, I didn't know she had been telling her students she was a socialist, although it didn't surprise me. It seemed to me the students should know her political bent if she was going to be teaching economic theory.

"Well, don't worry about it," she said. "I'm sure it'll pass, as all things must. George Harrison, remember? *'A cloudburst doesn't last all day.'* Administrators always get upset when professors stray from the norm."

I smiled, wondering if she realized how few parents quoted George Harrison to their teenage children. She made preparations for going to bed, but I sat on the couch a while, thinking about what might happen if she was fired. I worried too much, I knew, always preparing for the worst to happen. What had conditioned that in me, I wondered? Or was solicitude inherited like brown eyes? Finally, I went to bed myself. Not until several weeks later did I hear anything more about my mother's job. Meanwhile, I had several chances to get to know Cody even better than before.

Five

During the following weeks I saw virtually nothing of Christian or Flipping, for their band had entered a stage requiring hours and hours of rehearsal, confined in a rented warehouse in North Little Rock. Excepting a few uneventful meetings, Sarah had also disappeared from my life. It seemed our relationship had relaxed to a point of insignificance, and we were both relieved to put it on hold for a while.

Cody, on the other hand, increasingly involved himself with my life. At school, when not attending separate classes, more often than not we were together. Perhaps nowhere were we more closely associated with each other than in history class. Together we went 'round and 'round with Mrs. Kraemer, who would never concede that the United States had ever been on the wrong side of an issue. To her, our country and its government were absolutely perfect. Although nothing Cody and I could say was likely to change her mind, she at least let us say our piece.

One day she asked if anyone could tell her about the House Committee on Un-American Activities. Cody's hand was immediately in the air, a rebel asking permission to revolt. Mrs. Kraemer hesitated noticeably, but when no other hands were raised she was obliged to let Cody answer the question.

"It was a committee set up by Congress in 1938 for the purpose of engaging in Un-American Activities."

Mrs. Kraemer bristled. "It was a committee set up to help Americans get rid of all the communists and deviants."

I couldn't believe she actually said that. Behind me, Cody did a good job of maintaining his cool.

"I didn't realize that getting rid of people was what America was all about."

Mrs. Kraemer was looking smug, as if she could sense a victory.

"If it's necessary to protect the country, then you have to. The communists would destroy Christianity, and our forefathers came to this country to establish a Christian nation."

I'd heard about enough. "Our forefathers came to this country to escape religious persecution — at least some of them did," I said. "Unfortunately, many of them found it was much like going to South Africa to escape racism. Quakers used to be hanged on Boston Common — either that or tied to a cart and whipped from town to town, or have their ears cut off. And then, of course, there were the witches—"

"Stop it!"

The entire class was silent, and the laughter filtering in from a neighboring room seemed alien and impossible. Mrs. Kraemer, regaining her composure, said, "I did not give you permission to speak." On this minor point, she was correct.

"You just watch and see what the communists do," she urged the class. "Take a good long look at Central America — Nicaragua is now like Cuba when Castro first took over."

"I don't buy that for a minute," Cody said to me after class. "You might as well compare the Bolshevik Revolution with the American Revolution, the Stalin purges with our slaughter of the Indians, and their expansionism with our Manifest Destiny. You can draw as many comparisons as you want, but that doesn't mean Russia is going to someday turn into America. Neither will Nicaragua turn into Cuba — unless we force them to."

I agreed with him. "There must be a path between the U.S.

and Russia. A government should be able to take care of its people without oppressing them."

We had stopped at Cody's locker. He threw in two books and dug two others from the bottom of the heap.

"Don't you sometimes wonder, though, why so many revolutions are followed by dictatorships?"

"No," I said, "I never wonder. It's like wondering why *prosperous* comes just before *prostate* in a dictionary."

Cody laughed and shoved me away. "It is *not!* It's not the same thing at all!"

We continued our journey, heading back around a corner to my locker. I could overhear other conversations passing by, mostly concerning a football game which had been played over the weekend with our arch-rival. It seems a fight had broken out between the two teams. The students at our school obviously loved it. It was exciting having someone to hate.

"I was thinking just last night," Cody continued, "it sure would be funny if there was a full-scale nuclear war—"

I think I must have made some sound of disbelief, for Cody interrupted himself to silence me.

"No, just listen for a minute. We had a full-scale nuclear war, and all the bombs were duds! All 50,000 warheads, or whatever the figure is this week, they fire them all and nothing happens."

"I hope we never find out if they work or not."

We had arrived at my locker. I was wishing I had something else securing it other than a combination lock, which took a lot of time.

"Are you a pacifist?" Cody asked me.

I forgot where I was with the "four times to the right and stop at 63," and had to start over.

"What do you mean?" I asked.

"A pacifist. You know, you would never kill anybody under any circumstances."

"Oh, indeed I might! But I'd want to be selective about it. I would, for instance, need to know for sure it was in self-defense."

"If the Soviets were threatening us, you wouldn't fight them?"

I knew Cody was playing the devil's advocate, but this didn't make the question any easier.

"Just hold on a second. This killing people is a serious business. If I go off shooting every Russian who comes along, I could end up killing some very nice people. And *that* I'm totally opposed to — killing nice people."

Our conversation was halted by the threat of the approaching tardy bell.

In gym that afternoon Cody and I ended up on opposing football teams. Walking back to the huddle after the first play from scrimmage, Cody slapped me on the back and said, "Remember, you're a pacifist."

On the next play I tackled him so hard I was afraid I might have hurt him. He never said a word about it, but on the next play he sent this cute, dark-eyed boy to block me. I was sure I caught Cody grinning at me, a second before he threw a long pass downfield. In any case, I had this guy pawing me for the rest of the game, trying to keep me away from Cody.

I had begun to have this recurring dream in which I was in an underground shaft, running for my life it seemed, with electric lights whizzing by me, creating an unseen blur. All the while I was pursued by "X," the unknown, galloping through the outskirts of *nada*, with the sound of a mechanical, clicking beat echoing through the tunnel behind me, hot on my trail.

I had come to think my life was funneling inward to some central point, unknown to me, directly linked to Cody. While I felt satisfied the experience would be something positive, it really didn't matter much, for I had a habit of viewing my life as an outsider watching from a distance — and I would just as soon watch a good tragedy as a drama with a happy ending. That the story be interesting was all I asked.

A thread of melancholy from Camus' "The Renegade" was

frequently on Cody's tongue of late: *"Death too is cool, and it's shadow hides no god."* Then, one Saturday night at his brother-in-law's bar, Cody wrote a line of poetry which infiltrated my dreams:

DEATH — Passing silver trains at midnight in a sports car.

What worried me about my dreams was always being a passenger in the car, while Cody was always behind the wheel.

My hair had dried out from the morning shower in a peculiarly attractive wave. I felt good. I looked good. But everyone was busy — Cody at work, Flipping and Christian with practice, Freddy with some friend unknown to me. On Saturdays like this, I sometimes rode the buses.

The entertainment was sometimes in my head, games played with my eyelashes and the sun, making graphs of prejudice, stereotyping myself into probable causes, possible results.

Sometimes there was silent interplay with other passengers on the bus. An extremely grouchy couple got on with an incorrigibly charming little girl. The mother had apparently been rushed to catch the bus. As they walked down the aisle I heard her say to her husband, "Give me an aspirin and let me catch my breath!"

I'll try to find someone to give you a carload of death.

The husband gave her aspirin. I watched the little girl, whose happiness seemed to irritate her parents. They made futile attempts with threats at making her sad and when these didn't work, slapped her upside the head. Little girl, I thought, if you could see what they have in store for you, you would run away screaming.

I recall a story my mother told me of the early days after blacks no longer had to ride at the rear of buses. Some three years after the segregationist law had been discarded, Mom was waiting at a bus stop with a fellow student, who was black. When the bus arrived, Mom took a seat near the front, but her friend said she'd better go to the back. "They can't make you sit on the back of the bus," Mom told her. Her friend kept walking: "I know it, honey, but I sure feel safer when I do."

I usually sat at the back myself, as it was bouncier back there, reminding me slightly of a roller coaster. Young black males still rode at the back, I noted, but more for the privacy, I supposed. I would overhear things like "play both ends against the middle," but I didn't know what they meant.

Once I ran into Robert, of Robert and Val from Sarah's party. Walking down the aisle, he spotted me and sat down, calling me by name, then stating his before I had the chance to not remember, saving us both the embarrassment. He was boisterous, but nice. He held what appeared to be a poem he might have been reading while waiting on the bus. In a quick glance I saw it was written by Val, about her cat. Robert noticed the glance and asked if I'd like to read it. I replied that cat poems gave me asthma, only half in jest, but read it anyway. "Such little paws with teeny claws," I read, feeling my bronchial muscles contract.

And these were my Saturdays on the buses, drifting down roads oblique to my plans. These were the days I wanted to die the most.

Invariably, other Saturdays were spent with Cody, whenever he got a break from work, doing whatever. We drove up to Greers Ferry Lake one Saturday morning, a rather nice artificial reservoir to the north of Little Rock, in the foothills of the Ozarks. Up from one section of the lake rose a pinnacle of land. Cody and I paddled across to the pointed island in his father's fishing boat, which we brought along for this purpose. Cody had been quiet on the drive up, but it was early and his car's cassette deck kept us preoccupied with music, so I didn't think much about his silence. But once we were on the island, I began to notice he was in a strange mood. There was an overwhelming tension beneath his icy facade. It was hard to figure out, but then, I've never understood glaciers. He began our conversation with an anecdote about the Rolling Stones:

"Trotsky, I remember a line from some review of a Stones album which said they had not only outlived their usefulness, they'd outlived their uselessness as well—"

He stopped talking and started walking at the same time. Staring out across the water, he sat down. I snapped a weed in two, needing something to play with. I looked down at Cody, then followed his gaze across the water.

"What's so useless about your life?" I asked.

It wasn't a warm day. Waiting for Cody to answer, I watched the white smoky breath slipping from his coral-red lips.

"I just don't want to live the way other people live," he said, standing up.

"So don't."

"But that's just it! I don't know *how* I want to live. I can't think of a damn thing that interests me enough to base an entire life on."

I tried to think of something to say to this, but nothing came.

"Besides, sometimes I think death is more interesting. I want to know what happens next."

"It's just the explorer in you," I told him. "But what about exploring life? What happened to your intense desire to see frozen tundra?"

"Do you have to remember everything I say?"

"Would you rather I didn't?"

Cody didn't answer for a minute, then, with a smile, he said, "It's really rough, Trotsky. It really is."

I asked if he was talking about his life.

"No," he said. "I'm talking about being your friend."

We walked along the water's edge in silence, until we were halfway around the island from where we left the boat.

"You're not giving this death thing any serious consideration, are you?" I asked, trying to keep the caution out of my voice.

"Well, I do get curious about it sometimes."

"But you're going to die eventually anyway, so what's the rush?"

"I was just thinking I'd hate to wait until I was too old to enjoy it."

I was thankful for the opportunity to laugh, but could only manage a single chuckle.

"If you don't enjoy life, why should you want to keep living?" Cody asked.

"I guess most people do enjoy their lives. I thought you did, too."

"Do you?"

I started walking again to avoid his stare.

"I think I enjoy it most when I'm with you," I said. Cody didn't respond, but in a moment I felt his hand on my shoulder.

"You know," he said, "sometimes I think about the people of Chad or Ethiopia and I feel pain for them. But this pain I feel doesn't make me feel fortunate. There's nothing comparative about happiness, at least for me there isn't. Either I'm happy or I'm not, but I never feel *comparatively* happy." He stopped and turned me around to face him. "Am I making any sense?"

I retrieved a small, square piece of paper from my wallet and handed it over to Cody.

"Be courageous," he read aloud, *"for there is a divine purpose in living."* Cody handed the paper back to me. "Where did that come from?"

"From my last day in Lincoln. I was having lunch with these two guys I'd known from school, and I found this little message hanging down from my cup of tea."

"I didn't know you drank hot tea."

"Not often — it was a Chinese restaurant. But listen, Cody, you're missing the point."

"What is the point?"

He had removed his hand from my shoulder.

"The point is I still have it."

Cody looked at me suspiciously, then skipped a rock across the lake. We stood for a while, watching the ripple, until Cody said, "Too bad your tea bag doesn't elaborate."

I refused to respond to that, not knowing how to respond.

"Do you remember that night at the Magic Theatre?" I asked. Cody nodded. "Then you must realize how different what you're telling me now is from what you told me then. That night you were full of life, full of explanations for life — bodhisattvas, old souls, nirvana — I remember practically every word you said. And then there was the dream. And now. Now you're standing here telling me you want a tombstone that reads: 'STATION OFF. Please do not adjust set.'"

Cody smiled in spite of himself. "I remember, Trotsky — and I really do believe those things. It's just that I get so tired of getting tired sometimes, and I want to put my theories to the test, to see if my mind would expand once it escaped this body. Don't you ever think about it?"

"I've thought about it. I'm in no rush."

Yes, I had thought about it. I wondered if Cody had forgotten about me telling him of my non-accidental overdose.

It was not at all like a nightmare. It was the apex of some curve in courage I'd been striving for. Sure it was a time of depression, but it was also a time when I had been thinking about life more than at any other period, a time of wonder, a time of intense curiosity, and even of revenge. Sometimes you get too lonely, and this can happen even if you have the best of parents, the best of friends. Sometimes you are not willing to expend the effort. Sometimes you wish to move on, hopefully to something better. So you say to the gods, "I don't have to take this," and you swallow eighty times at least, then let the numbness sink in. But it is numbness mixed with exhilaration, oh what a dream, heroin with a difference. But there are always things left undone, unnerving questions, also fear. Guns probably do work better, but you cannot allow an object you despise to kill you. In any case you feel it will soon be okay. Let sleep come quickly. Please.

I can't describe the feeling of mind and body separation I felt, so intense it seemed a shame people couldn't live that way, feeling that sensation, all the time. I began to drift off into many trains of thought, wondering, in passing, which thought would be my last. The drugs had finally done their trick, allowing me to float through this, fear no longer in control. I wondered if the thoughts would simply end or change from conscious to unconscious thoughts and then to something else. The one thought that could sober me even in this condition was that of my family: my mother and Freddy. I knew I was doing something terrible to them, and the guilt was impossible to deal with, sobering through four hundred milligrams of anything. I lay there, waiting, like I always had, for something to happen . . . listening, as it were, to an English band called The Cure.

For some strange reason I did not die. But I couldn't exactly wake up, either, and this had frightened Freddy into calling for help.

Cody began skipping rocks across the surface of the lake. The stiff wind coming off the water made this simple task difficult.

"I'm so goddamn sick of working in that service station!" he said, raising himself to his full height. "Last year it was an auto parts store, this year a service station. I don't even like cars! Why should I have to be their doctor?"

"Well, you're certainly moving *across* in the world, aren't you?" I said, hoping it would bring a smile. It almost worked. Cody quickly snapped his eyes in my direction, but just as quickly snapped them back toward the lake.

"If I could just not feel so anxious. That's what I always liked about marijuana — it relaxed me, made me less uptight. But now that doesn't work for me either."

"My mother tells me growing old is the best depressant around."

This time Cody did crack a smile. "Every kid should have a mom like yours," he said.

"It helps," I had to admit. I had met Cody's parents recently and had not been impressed. I could see why he didn't like them, as they were perhaps the most singularly unlikable middle-aged couple I'd ever met. It's amazing how anyone like Cody could come from such a creepy family. His older brother was the worst of all. Possessing none of Cody's good looks and even less of his charm, Kenny seemed to go about life as if he were king and the rest of humanity existed merely to please him. His egocentrism was in evidence throughout their house; when I had first entered the place, my first question was, "Who's Kenny?" There were Kenny coffee mugs, Kenny towels in the bathroom, and plastic labels spelling out Kenny Cody which were stuck on various objects around the house — even to certain books on the family bookshelf. By the time we met, I already hated Kenny, and seeing him in person only made it worse. His name actually *was* Kenny — not Kenneth or Ken. I could not imagine anyone naming their children Kenny and Washington Damon unless they were trying to force the first into show business and the latter into making useful products from peanuts.

I remember my surprise at seeing Cody's room for the first time. Although immaculately clean, it was totally lacking in decorative objects save one poster from the 1980 Presidential campaign, reading "Re-Elect President Carter." Otherwise, the room was the bland and nondescript cell of a college dorm before the students move in.

Cody grabbed me around the neck and began walking along the shore. I noticed lately he was allowing himself to be more and more physical with me. During the last few days I could recall one occasion when he patted me good-naturedly on the cheek, another when he snuck up behind me, grabbed me around the chest and squeezed the living daylights out of me ("living daylights" I picked up from my mom — don't know what it means literally, but I sure like the sound of it), and here he was now grabbing me around the neck, walking along the shore of our mountain island in full view of several distant fisherpeople. For me, his physical presence was intoxicating. I never wanted anything as much in my life as I wanted him, wanted to reach over and grab him, kiss him, pull him down into the milkweed and make out for hours. But I gave no hint of my desires, for I was not so sure they were shared desires, was not at all certain the warmth exuding from Cody was a product of the same fire that made me flush with passion, left me feverish with longing. At times I felt guilty for not being completely satisfied just having Cody as my friend.

When we got back into town that evening we found my mother camped out on the living room floor, a bowl of chips and hot cheese dip at her side, reading, oddly enough, *The Plague*, by Camus. I knew she had read it several times, but I couldn't remember her having read anything by Camus in the last few years. Since he had lately been reading Camus to the limit, Cody thought it was a wonderful coincidence.

I went in the kitchen to fix us some orange juice, so I missed the first part of the conversation. When I returned, Cody was saying, "That statement he made about suicide being the only true philosophical question sticks with me. I believe he was on target, don't you?"

Mom answered with some amount of premeditation evident in her words, as if, perhaps in her classes and certainly in her own mind, she had been over this point before.

"That is the *essential* question. When you come face to face with what Camus called 'the absurdity of the universe,' then you must decide whether or not you want to put up with it. But if you decide to live, then you must decide *how* you are going to live."

Cody regarded her with the same expression he always gave me when keenly interested in something I had said. He continued her thought process, saying, "But once you have realized the absurdity of the universe, its indifference to man, then you can make a commitment, to give your life meaning — at least insofar as the commitment gives you a purpose for being. I remember reading in Camus that the only way to be free is to free yourself of others, especially the institutions and ideologies of society."

I joined the conversation. "But in *The Plague* Camus seems to say it is better to have the plague — that is, to be caught up in society — than to be isolated. So how do you free yourself from others without becoming isolated?"

"That's an excellent question," Mom said. "Have either of you ever heard of a man named John Stuart Mill?"

We shook our heads.

"He was an English philsospher, and also an economist, which is how I know of him. He is believed to have had the highest I.Q. in all of history."

"That's a pretty sweeping statement."

"Yes, I know," Mom said, smiling."But that's what's said of him. In any case, he believed that the goal of any society should be to provide the greatest amount of happiness for the greatest number of people."

"Marxism in a nutshell."

"In a way, yes. Specifically, it's utilitarianism. But it was Camus' ideas of social theory which first attracted me to his work. Camus was a Marxist in terms of conscience, which is where it does the most good, in my view. Marx said, 'Until all men are free, no men are free.' Camus believed commitments should be aimed at freeing others, making them aware of the absurdity of the world so they can make meaningful commitments toward improving it. The liberator must dip into the plague in order to free the captives, but you should work with something you love, something you can believe in and pursue with passion."

"But that still doesn't answer my question," I persisted. "How do you free yourself from others without becoming an isolationist?"

"You free yourself from the influence and expectations of others, of society, yet you remain a physical part of that society in order to instigate change within it, freeing others. It's two different steps."

Cody grinned at her, then directed his attention to me. "It's the same concept as the bodhisattva, except on a less spiritual level."

I had been thinking the same thought.

"Well, I'm going to bed," Mom announced. "Goodnight Cody. Trotsky."

"Goodnight."

"'Night Mom."

Cody and I decided to continue our conversation in my room, where we could listen to music.

"Did you ever go to church when you were younger?" I asked Cody.

"Sure. All the time. It was an Assembly of God church, and I'll never forget the preacher. He was very short, but had this booming voice, and he used to read scriptures from the King James version, emphasizing all the words in italics. You should pick up a Bible and try it sometime. It's hilarious."

"Do you ever wonder if there really is a God?" I asked then, thinking back to the terrifying nightmare which had recently shaken me.

"Why do you ask?"

"It's just that sometimes I wonder, that's all."

"Well, if there is, he must be a bloody sadist."

"Either that or powerless."

"I don't believe in anything, if you want to know the truth."

"Agnostic, huh?"

"Yes."

"The unknown is unknowable. Makes sense to me, too."

"So how do you live for, oh, say seventy years, if you believe that?"

"Day to day, I would think."

"What's the use?"

"Wasn't that Camus' *second* philosophical question?"

"Far as I know he only had one."

"Do you think it does any good to pray, or meditate?"

"Well, thinking can be good or evil, and that's all prayer or meditation are, aren't they? Just thinking through what you want, what mistakes you've made, things you've done that violated your conscience. I would guess you're actually asking yourself for forgiveness, wouldn't you?"

"I don't know."

"Exactly. The perfect agnostic answer. I suppose we're going to pretend we prayed to meet each other? That we meditated to have parallel dreams? No, those things just happen. There seems to be no design to the spiritual realm — at least nothing you can be sure of."

"Maybe it really is predestined."

"Maybe we'll never know."

When Cody took his leave, I stood on the front porch watching his car disappear down the street. Sometimes I wished they still made cars with running boards. It would be such fun to have someone you love pulling off down the road, and to hop on the running board and smile at them for half a block.

I wondered if Cody would ever spend the night with me again. Although he hadn't since that first time, I wasn't going to worry about it; the friendship was intense enough to perpetually whet my interest. If Cody did not feel comfortable in bed with me, he at least did not let it prevent us from becoming best friends.

Sometime around midnight, Freddy came in from a night of bike riding, sweaty and exhilarated. I knew he had made some friends around the neighborhood, but I hadn't made the effort to see who any of them were. Watching him gulp down a sixteen-ounce cola, I longed to relive those physically active days he was passing through ... days I must have outgrown when I wasn't looking. I remember riding my spider bike around the streets and through the fields surrounding our house. There were trails everywhere, with nice bumps to sail over and shallow creek beds to cross. I loved to pop wheelies, do skids, ride no-hands forever, and occasionally get hurt attempting the impossible. One could imagine oneself to be anybody, anything.

Freddy was telling me about some vacant house a few blocks away which he and a friend named Mark had been exploring. He said there were a lot of plastic bags and tubes of model cement lying around the place, which certainly didn't surprise me. I asked if he knew what that was all about and he said he did, so I warned him not to hang around there, because people get crazy when they sniff glue and he could easily find himself in a dangerous situation if he stumbled across them at the wrong time. If I didn't know whether Freddy would follow my advice or not, I knew he wasn't stupid. He hadn't given me any reason to worry about him in the past, so I wasn't going to start now.

Freddy settled down in front of the television to watch a science-fiction movie, familiar from my childhood, in the days when I had tried my hardest to stay awake for "Chiller," a Saturday night movie series that came on at ten-thirty. It was hard to believe I once had trouble staying awake until midnight, but I could remember that being the case.

Leaving Freddy to the television, and taking refuge in my room, I played my stereo at a low volume and looked through some magazines I had picked up recently. Later, after going to bed and not falling asleep, I was about to turn on a light to read some more when I thought I heard a faint noise coming from Freddy's room. Uncertain if I was really hearing something, I decided to get up and check it out.

When I opened Freddy's door, I heard him turn to face away from me. It was too dark to see anything but the vague outlines of unidentifiable shapes, so I stood at the door and waited. Then I heard a small, childlike sob, so I gingerly made my way across the anarchy of Freddy's cluttered floor and sat at the side of his bed.

"What's wrong?" I asked, putting a hand on his shoulder.

"Nothing," he said through his tears, as a cold shiver ran the length of his body. I was reminded of a line from *Siddhartha:* *"He shivered inwardly like a small animal, like a bird or a hare, when he realized how alone he was."*

"Come on, tell me what's the matter."

There was a long silence, which I expected. Freddy had a difficult time putting his feelings into words, so I knew that even if he wanted to tell me what was bothering him, it would be a while before he could.

After a time, he said, "Some nights I just lay here and feel frightened and I don't know why."

If he only knew how hard that hit home. I remembered back to the nights when I myself had lain in bed gripped by some unknown terror. Many times these bouts with fear occurred when there was some trauma in my life, like the night before my first day at a new school. But the trauma never equaled the terror, and at other times the terror occurred without any outside instigation. I played back Freddy's words several times in my mind: "Sometimes I just feel frightened and I don't know why."

"Everyone does," I told him, trying to be big-brother reassuring, knowing he would probably fall for it like he always did, but conscious also of the approaching day when I would fall from Freddy's grace for not being the infallible god he had always thought me to be. I wondered if what I was telling him was true. *Did* everyone feel that terror at some point in their lives? I didn't feel I had sufficient data regarding life to know if my feelings and my family's experience strayed far from the American norm. Something told me they probably did, and that perhaps I should be grateful they did, but for the moment I was willing to assume they did not if it would give Freddy some peace of mind. I didn't know what else to tell him.

When Freddy turned to face me, I could see the moisture covering his face, betraying remnants of a good cry. I reached over and wiped away the Judas tears, feeling as protective as I ever would, and feeling as good about myself, and about Freddy, as I was ever likely to feel. This boy, my younger brother, was more than my life to me. I wasn't sure I had ever told Freddy I loved him, because what I felt was much stronger than words. Anything I could have said to him would have seemed a sacrilege. He was lying flat on his back, staring at me, as I wiped away his tears. Then I pushed the hair back off his forehead and smiled at him, hoping he would smile back at me. It worked like magic.

"You know," Freddy said, obviously having to search for

his words, "sometimes it's like you're my father. I learn things from watching you, and that helps out. Then I wonder sometimes how you manage, without someone older than you leading the way. It makes me glad you're the oldest."

He had never said anything quite like this to me before, and I wasn't sure why he was saying it now. In any case, I thought he had said it exceptionally well, and I tried to be just as reflective in my reply.

"You can learn things, feel your way through. You just look around you, see what's going on, then pick out what's real for yourself. If there's something you need to know, you can ask someone or try to find the answer in a book. But sometimes it would've been easier having a father. Masturbation was certainly a trauma."

"Yeah, thanks for warning me about that one."

"No problem."

Freddy was silent for a few minutes, and I could almost tell what he was thinking. Finally, he asked, "Have you ever done it with anyone, Trotsky?"

It wasn't an easy question to answer, and it didn't escape my attention that he had used the word "anyone" and not "a girl." I wondered how much he already suspected, and also wondered if he was going to follow me along this road, too. I sincerely hoped he would not, although I wasn't quite sure why. Maybe I just felt our mother deserved some grandchildren from one of us.

"I'd rather not answer that one."

"Why not?"

"I just like to have a few secrets nobody knows but me."

"But I'll tell you whenever I do."

"Will you, though?" I asked teasingly.

"Sure I will. Now tell me!"

"Get some sleep. You seem to be feeling better now."

Freddy gave up with a sigh.

"Ya know," he said, "life sure is different after you reach thirteen."

"It just keeps getting stranger," I agreed.

Freddy turned over again, yawning widely. "Thanks for coming in," he said. "Talking to you always helps."

"No problem," I said, as much to myself as to him. "See you in the morning."

Six

Keenly interested in the latest discoveries and theories in astronomy, I sat in on a lecture given by an astronomer from Texas' McDonald Observatory. He claimed that if a large telescope, powerful enough to see forty billion light years away, could be stationed in space, far from the interference of the earth's atmosphere, astronomers could theoretically watch the birth of the universe, which they estimated to have exploded into existence some forty billion years ago.

I thought of the ancient Norse belief that the earth was cut and shaped from the body of Ymir, father of the frost giants and enemy of the gods. I thought of the human sacrifices made to the Phoenician god, Moloch; of the Aztec's dedication of the great pyramid temple in Tenochtitlan, when the Aztec chiefs and priests slit open the bodies and tore out the hearts of twenty thousand captives to appease the gods; of the Sumerian belief that man was created from the blood of the dragon Tiamat, mother of Chaos. The Sumerians gradually disappeared as a people, burying their gods with them.

I had long been fascinated by ancient religions, and was often left feeling melancholy as I put down a book about the worship and sacrifice, the hope and devotion, of some ancient people who had been just as sure they knew the "truth" as the fundamentalists are today.

My exploration of religion did not rest solely in dead gods, however, for I was continually aware of the supernatural element in my own life. Often I wondered if someday I might succeed in tapping the curious energy that dreamed those dreams, that made coincidence a commonplace occurrence in my life. Cody was at the center of all these dreams and mysticisms, leaving me to believe the answer lay in some chemistry between us, though I could never pinpoint it further. Since I could not put my faith in anything else, I trusted in and tried to honor my own intuitions and conscience, leading me to an individualistic, situation ethic with which I was pleased. Although my good and evil applied only to myself, I felt the world might show improvement if my ethics were more universally applied.

Commitment continued to elude me. I could not imagine dying like my father for the faceless masses. Had they, I wondered, seemed less faceless to him? Certainly, my mother seemed to share his commitment. However, having grown just as weary of political arguments as I had of philosophical diatribes, I was no more inclined to die for the social democrats than I was for the logical positivists.

Meanwhile, there was twentieth-century Arkansas providing me with plenty of questions. It took quite a bit of effort to make it through school, through sidewalks, through conversations, when all around was talk of hunting and deer season, talk of cars, and the inevitable racist slurs. Often I felt like talking to no one, but as I began to sink into myself, it seemed the world took a greater interest in my plans. I could understand when the questions came from my peers, for they were searching out ideas for their own lives. But when every adult who had any small claim of knowing me asked these questions, I wondered if they were comparing the career plans of their own children with "others of that age group." I could envision their minds running something like this: "So you haven't made a decision? Well, our Teddy plans to study accounting. We had hoped for something like law, or maybe engineering, but at least he has decided on something, which is more than you've done, isn't it?"

If it had not been for Cody, I would have been miserable living in Little Rock. Even with Cody there was seldom much to do that was entertaining. Coming home from a night of drinking with Cody, I would look in the bathroom mirror and hardly recognize myself, often shocked by the dullness of my own eyes. Partly it was the drink, and partly it was the weariness from my search for purpose, a pursuit which lately had centered more and more on my love for Cody. *For what other straws were even worth grasping at? Answer, me, that.*

Cody had lived in Little Rock all his life, had grudgingly learned how to act the part of the Arkansas male. The times I saw him performing this role took my by surprise. The idea that he could slip into characterizations so easily made me uneasy, but I didn't think he would ever do it to deceive me.

I would like to have seen photographs, diaries, anything of Cody's past, but his family had kept no photographs, not even the usual school pictures, and Cody had kept no records: no diary, no scrapbook, no favorite toys. Cody was concerned with the future and the present. Cody two years ago, Cody at ten, Cody in the second grade, were as far removed from him as the lives of Nauruan phosphate miners.

It was eerie knowing someone who had retained so little from his past, but I chose to honor all our differences, often respecting his variances more than my own. It wasn't Cody that worried me, it was my own special talent for thinking about everything that made me weary. At times I wanted to tear my brain out and slap it around a bit. I could never be as strong as my intellect told me I should be. In the end, what would it matter? Why did trivialities ever cause me a minute's worry? When confronted with my fanatical bouts of depression as a child, my mother had often said to me, "Trotsky, what could it matter to a solar system?" I still thought of that from time to time, and frequently it helped. At other times nothing helped.

One day I came home to find another golden boy in our house. He was in the kitchen with Freddy, apparently making some peanut butter sandwiches. They were both sweaty and I could easily detect that unique odor that comes from fourteen-year-old boys when they perspire. I said hello to Freddy, then looked at the new kid. Since Freddy didn't offer an introduction, I said, "My name's Trotsky. Who're you?"

"Mark," he told me. "I'm in Freddy's class at school."

There didn't seem to be anything more to say, so I didn't say anything. I never was much at making small talk with Freddy's friends. I clicked on the black-and-white TV on the counter, then spread out some of my books on the bar at the other end, thinking I'd get my homework out of the way in case something I wanted to do came up later.

"Are you sure you aren't hungry?" Freddy asked Mark.

"Not really. I'll just drink a Coke and watch you eat."

"Okay, but my eating habits aren't that entertaining."

"You might be surprised," I said, without looking up from my book.

"Funny, Trotsky," Freddy said sarcastically. There was another silence as I read, Freddy ate, and Mark watched him. Mark eventually broke the silence by asking what grade I was in.

"I'm a senior," I said.

"I told you that already," Freddy said to Mark. I glanced up, saw Mark staring at me, then tried again to concentrate on my lessons.

"You must be a good student," he said. I looked up again, just briefly, smiled at him, and muttered something to the effect that I got by.

"Come on, let's go," Freddy said, grabbing Mark and heading for the door.

"Hey, how 'bout putting those in the dishwasher," I said, indicating their dirty glasses and knives. Freddy performed this task quickly, then they left.

"See ya 'round," Mark said on his way out the door.

I hesitated just a moment after the door was shut then went to the front window and looked from a distance through an opening in the curtains. I saw them get on their bikes, pop wheelies, circle each other indecisively, then race off down the street. I tried to analyze what I was feeling, finally having to reprimand myself: "No way, Trotsky, he's too young!"

But Mark sort of blew into my life in a whirlwind. Soon he was spending every afternoon with Freddy, and I saw him not only in passing, but also in participation, whenever they needed me for something like cards or football, or to take them someplace in my car. I tried to accommodate them as much as possible, well remembering what a pain it was having to depend on others for distant transportation. It seemed to me almost from the first that Mark had a private and singular interest in me, and it didn't take me long to guess the nature of his interest.

Mark was tall for his age, had a full shock of blond hair, and possessed the sort of square shoulders you usually don't see on boys until they reach sixteen or so. His eyebrows were full, especially for a blond, and his eyes were chocolate brown. When he laughed, his mouth seemed to take up the greater part of his face, giving the impression he was one big open-mouthed grin. His voice obviously had been changing for some time now, for it had settled into that sort of deep rasp which I've always found strangely sensuous and comforting. As far as clothes went, Mark wasn't particularly different from the general male adolescent population — jeans, flannel shirts, sweatshirts, pullover sweaters, all mostly in blues and browns, although in Arkansas you encountered more than the usual amount of red, as well. The only thing striking me as unusual about Mark's manner of dressing was that it seemed to call attention to himself as a physical being. Generally, his shirt was unbuttoned — at least the top two-thirds — and he always wore a plain silver chain around his neck, a medallion of sorts, which had a small strip of leather tied tightly around it at the middle. Mark also never wore underwear. I might not have noticed this if he had not supplied me with constant opportunities. When I played football with them, for instance, it was sometimes fairly obvious. Once I asked if he wasn't afraid he might hurt himself.

He smiled, as if to confirm he knew what I meant, but he didn't answer. Another time, when Mark was spending the night with Freddy, he had taken a shower, then joined us in the living room to watch television. Wearing nothing but a pair of cut-off shorts, he positioned himself between us with his legs sort of flung out in my direction. Every time he said something to me and I looked over at him, I could clearly see up one of his cut-offs legs — and it was abundantly clear he was wearing no underwear. I forced myself to believe this performance was unintentional.

But Mark constantly was talking to me, coming into my room to see what I was doing, and just generally concerning himself with my business far more than any of Freddy's friends had in the past. I liked him a lot, thought he was fun to be around, and I must admit I was flattered by all his attention.

Freddy and I started another hockey league, with Mark a full participant. Cody played sometimes as well, but he wasn't around enough to develop his talent to the same extent as Freddy and I. Mark, on the other hand, quickly became our equal, spending many a night with us fiercely engaged in battle with the little hockey men. From the beginning of time I had been Montreal and Freddy had been New York, the two "glamour" teams by anyone's standards, with the other four teams switching owners from year to year. Mark found an empathy with Toronto, and whenever the two Canadian teams went at it, things were especially interesting. We beat each other to death while Freddy took New York to the championship. While Freddy's New York team didn't lose a game, his other team (Detroit) didn't win a game. But Freddy had always been like that.

All of my worries and concerns in life were so embryonic in Mark's development, his presence was a welcome challenge to smile for a change. I noticed, too, that Freddy was considerably happier these days, now that Mark had become his closest friend.

Like I said, Mark sort of blew into my life in a whirlwind,

and one Saturday night when he was staying over with Freddy, as he did just about every Saturday, the direction of our relationship became clear. I came in from an evening with Cody (we had seen a Peter Weir double-header, then spent a couple of hours discussing the films at one of the sandbars on the Arkansas River) finding Freddy asleep on the living room floor and Mark lying on the couch, still watching the end of a movie on cable TV. For some reason all sense of caution abandoned me, and I casually walked over to the couch and sat down on top of Mark. He was wearing only his cut-offs, as usual, but had wrapped himself in a blanket. I was still wearing my heavy coat, which was even a bit damp from whatever misty substance was blowing around outside. Mark immediately broke into that infectious grin of his, and he grabbed my hands, most likely to prevent me from tickling him.

"You're cold," he said, looking at me as if he were trying to figure out what I was going to do next before I did it. I just sat there, pretended for a moment to be checking out the movie, then slowly moved one of my frosty hands underneath the blanket, making a cold, imaginary line from the top of his chest to his navel. Just as I thought would happen, I began to feel him getting hard.

What happened next was fairly incredible. Below the blanket, Mark took my hand and moved it farther down his body, to rest on his cut-offs. All the time, he continued to stare at me, laughing.

"Aren't you gonna take your coat off?" he asked, sounding a bit more mature than I had expected.

I stood up to remove the coat, but when I started to sit down again Mark brought himself up to a sitting position and moved over to the back of the couch. Still wrapped in the blanket, he held one end of it out for me to crawl under. I thought about it a minute, then looked back at the television.

"You want to see the rest of this?" I asked him.

"Not really," he said.

I calculated the risk — my mother in her bedroom, Freddy

asleep on the floor — then asked, "You want to go to my room?"

Mark nodded his head and got up from the couch.

"Should I turn off the TV?" he asked.

"No, just leave it on."

In my bedroom we wasted no time at all getting into bed. I had to undress, but Mark was practically nude already. His body really was well-built for a fourteen-year-old. Too, there was something about his boyish innocence that was definitely a turn-on — to me, at least. Mark wasn't the most beautiful of boys, but he was cute, and he was fun, and I liked him.

"Is this the first time you've done this?" I asked.

"No," he answered.

"Lots of times?"

He nodded yes. "Since I was twelve, usually with the guy who lives next door to me."

And who could this fellow be, I wondered to myself.

"Red Stanley. You probably go to school with him."

I had not expected to get a name, much less one I'd heard before.

"Yes, I've heard his name," I said, for it was true that although I had heard Christian and Flipping curse him enough, I had yet to meet the guy in person. I guessed I had probably seen him around school not knowing who he was. Small world, I was thinking, just as Mark said the most astonishing thing:

"Red's okay, I guess, but as soon as I saw you, I knew I could do better."

"Thanks," I said, meaning it. "You're not so bad yourself."

"Thanks," Mark said.

I knew he was waiting for me to lead us wherever I willed, but I had no clear idea where this would be. Although he might not have guessed, I imagined he was infinitely more experienced with this sort of thing than I, even though I was three years his senior. What I really wanted to do was kiss him, but I had gathered from several sources that while many boys his age didn't mind having sex with you, they weren't interested in the more intimate side of it. I decided to kiss him anyway, and although he seemed surprised, he not only went along but was soon encouraging it and taking the lead.

"I'm glad you don't smoke," he said at length. I wondered if this meant Stanley *did* smoke. It was annoying to be compared with others when making love. I suppose this is one reason people find virgins so appealing.

I kissed him again, then Mark began to take control, surprising me with the direction he was taking us. I kissed his face repeatedly while he encircled me with his legs and pressed me tight against him. He put some kind of grip on me the likes of which I've never felt since, biting me on the shoulder, on my arm, clutching me so hard I was in pain, but didn't care. I can't say I've ever been happier in my life than I was in the next few minutes: This unexpected blond boy nibbling at my shoulder, his arms clutched tightly 'round my neck, and me just barely retaining consciousness.

Afterwards, we lay on our backs, Mark's head in the crook of my arm, staring at a blank ceiling. "So you enjoyed that?" I asked, noticing his surprise at the question.

"Depends on who's doing it. I didn't like it when Stanley tried to get me to at first, but then I got used to it." Then, as an afterthought, "But I don't let Stanley do it anymore."

"Good," I told him, giving him another kiss. "Where did you do it, anyway? At his house?"

"No, there's a vacant house not far from here that you can get into easily. We met there sometimes."

I thought about Freddy's story about the vacant house and tubes of glue.

"You and Stanley don't sniff glue, do you?" I asked.

"Did Freddy tell you about the house?"

"Yes, he said he went there with you — only I didn't know who you were at the time."

"Yeah, Stanley's into glue. And he would get me high sometimes before he . . . you know."

Now I was disgusted. I took Mark in my arms and looked

into his eyes. "Promise me something, Mark. Don't have sex with Stanley anymore, okay? And even more important, don't be sniffing glue. It's too dangerous. Will you promise me you won't do it anymore?"

Mark turned away from me. "You're not my father, you know."

"I don't want to be your father."

Mark was silent for several minutes. I could see his eyes staring at the ceiling.

"I've already quit getting it on with Stanley, so you don't have to worry about that. But I like getting high."

What a shame, I was thinking. But I couldn't stop him, and I had said all I knew to say to talk him out of it. I did have another concern, however.

"Has Freddy been involved in any of this?"

Mark looked at me as if I suddenly had become the enemy, and I suppose it *was* stupid of me to think he would tell on his best friend.

"No, he hasn't," Mark said. "He doesn't know anything about Stanley, and he doesn't know I've done glue, either. He had his chance to try it, but he acted like the idea shocked him, so I made it look like I was just teasing."

We stared at each other.

"Do you believe me?" Mark asked.

"Yes, I believe you."

"Good."

That first time in bed with Mark is about the closest thing to S&M I've ever experienced. It was easy to see why, once I thought about it later. I hadn't the experience to lead, so Mark had taken over and assumed he could please me best by letting me do to him what Stanley liked to do. And it had worked, for the most part. I *did* enjoy it, and if I hadn't exactly been in love with Mark before, I certainly was afterwards. But there was also something about it — the pain, to be precise — which bothered me. As my sexual experiences with Mark became rather commonplace in the following weeks, this was gradually eliminated from our acts of passion. Before long I had convinced Mark to swear off glue, but I was just as addicted to sex as he was.

Sunday morning my mother awoke in her bedroom, I awoke in my bedroom, Mark awoke in Freddy's bedroom, and Freddy awoke on the living room carpet. I didn't have to look in the mirror to know what kind of red mark I'd have on my neck. Luckily, nobody but Mark had been up when I got in that night, and it was a Sunday, so I would have a day for the thing to fade before I'd have to show my face at school. Freddy picked up on something, however. I'm not sure if it was a look I gave Mark, or perhaps Mark even told him — but whatever it was, I knew Freddy probably figured out what was going on, or at least had a pretty good idea. I was never sure if Freddy and Mark's relationship ever crossed the border from friends to lovers. It certainly was a lot simpler for Mark to sleep with Freddy than for him and me to find the right time and place for love. But if they did have their moments, neither of them ever said a word about it to me, and I didn't care to ask them. Now it's just one of many things I'll never know about my brother and his best friend, and certainly not the most important. What I would really like to know is what they would have grown into, what they would have looked like and acted like when they were eighteen ... or twenty-five ... or forty. I wonder if Mark and I would have had a chance as lovers in this old world, or if we would have eventually grown apart. I could have even ended up in prison, since our lovemaking was criminal under Arkansas law, and seventeen-year-olds are tried as adults. Possibly, Mark would have married eventually, had kids of his own, and remembered me only as an adolescent crush. Those are some of the things I'll never know about those two. But only a few of them.

Seven

The first major front of the season was moving in, with an uproar of swirling leaves and banging gates, signaling that fall would soon become winter. Before its path, communities of blackbirds scurried farther south. If you knew what to look for, it was one of the most exciting days of the year. I was sitting in the kitchen drinking coffee and preparing to read the paper, but was distracted by the view through the sliding glass doors of the birds swooping to the ground and back in and out of trees, a neighbor's dog giving the occasional chase, ragweed shooting up into the air as if gravity was being selective on this, the freest of days.

I had decided I liked autumn in Arkansas. Located where both conifers and deciduous trees thrive, the hills were thick with a wide variety of trees, especially beautiful in the fall, with millions of leaves changing colors: birch, elm, redbud, dogwood, hickory, several kinds of oak, the cottonwood and cypress along the creek banks, the brilliant yellow leaves of the sweet gum, and the equally beautiful red of the maple and sumac. I loved walking at dusk through the woods and fields near our house, enjoying the sunset, as the wind picked up and temperatures fell rapidly, listening to the bobwhites and whippoorwills singing their names, the cawing of the crows, and the ever-present barking of distant dogs. After the first frost you could walk just about anywhere in the woods without too much worry of getting ticks and chiggers. Even on rainy days the walks were nice, for there was an edge of excitement in the air as folks shook off the summer sluggishness common to people throughout the South.

Finally, I turned my attention to the newspaper, startled by the first thing to catch my eye. In the lower right-hand corner of the front page was a photo of my mother, with the accompanying headline: "Professor Warned to Cut Comments on Socialism." I read the article slowly, allowing each sentence to circle around in my brain several times before going on to the next.

Ms. Helen Trottingham Taylor, an assistant professor of economics at the University of Arkansas at Little Rock and a member of the Democratic Socialists of America, has been directed by the school administration to stop informing her students at the beginning of each semester that she is a socialist.

Chancellor Neyland Rushent gave the order after meeting with other university officials over the weekend. The request came after the administration received several complaints from students about Ms. Taylor's pronouncements.

Rushent said he considered Ms. Taylor's practice unnecessary and in the long run educationally harmful.

"A point of view is going to come across eventually," he said. "But the learning process is more open if a point of view is not enunciated."

Contacted at her home Monday night, Ms. Taylor disagreed, saying, "As a professor of economic theory, I am giving many students their first exposure to various schools of thought in economics. Although I make every attempt to do this as objectively as possible, I feel my views as a socialist may color some of the information I impart. Therefore, I feel it is important to inform the students of my political bent early in the semester, before it would cost them money to change classes."

Ms. Taylor said she would not make a decision regarding compliance with the directive until she had discussed the situation with lawyers from the American Civil Liberties Union, and with local representatives of the American Association of University Professors.

Dr. Clive Elliot, president of the UALR branch of the AAUP, said the groups would meet Tuesday night to discuss the situation.

I wondered why I had not been told about this last night, then recalled I had been out past midnight and had missed seeing "Ms. Taylor." With difficulty, since my stomach was knotting up, I finished my coffee and skimmed through the rest of the paper, plasticoating my day with the usual dose of stories on world traumas, while waiting for Mom to get out of the shower.

Finally, I heard the bathroom door open. Approaching her with the paper in hand, I motioned to the article and asked how she was feeling.

"Angry," she said. "I never thought they would take it this far, though I should have foreseen it, knowing UALR."

"But I thought you liked the school."

"I do like it. My students are bright kids and classes tend to be interesting. The school administration isn't all that bad either, but they're exceedingly paranoid. As a public institution they have to be receptive to the views of the surrounding community, which in this case includes the state legislature. I understand there's been some threat of a lawsuit, but the press hasn't picked up on it yet.

"A suit against you?"

"I'm not sure. I think against the school, forcing them to fire me."

"Can they do that? Legally, I mean?"

"I've tried to research it, but the constitution of this state is a labyrinth of hogwash. The only legal ground I could find for them was a statute saying it's against the law for state employees to advocate the violent overthrow of the U.S. government, or to join subversive organizations — and it specifically mentions the Communist Party or its affiliates. So I guess they would have to prove the DSA is a subversive organization, which it's not.

"Isn't there some law about academic freedom, a guarantee of free speech, or something?"

"Well, there's the Bill of Rights, of course, but states have founds ways of disregarding that precious document ever since 1791, when it was added to the Constitution."

I was standing at the door of her bathroom watching as she brushed her hair. She was wearing a dark blue robe and holding some silver clip pins, which she placed in her mouth from time to time when she needed both hands.

"I don't really think much'll come of this. They're not about to make me a martyr."

And she smiled and I smiled back. I thought about her for most of the day. Not only had she got herself through some tough situations in the past, she had pulled Freddy and me through some as well. And now, a new challenge.

Whenever I picked up a paper or turned on the local news during the next few days, I would see something about Mom. Twenty-three members of the Arkansas legislature threatened a suit seeking to have her removed from her teaching position. One said he would oppose all appropriations for the university until she was dismissed. Letters to the editors of the *Arkansas Gazette* and *Arkansas Democrat* began appearing daily, with most readers, particularly in the *Democrat*, expressing outrage over taxpayers' money being used to pay the salary of an admitted "red." At school, total strangers were asking me if the Ms. Taylor who taught at the university was my mother. When I said she was, they generally replied with something like, "Figured she might be, being a commie." On one of these occasions, Cody almost intervened with his fists, but I managed to convince him it wasn't worth it. Freddy, however, wasn't so fortunate, arriving home from school Friday afternoon with torn clothes and a black eye.

While there were voices of support, they tended to be drowned out by all the yahoos wanting Mom's head. The ACLU agreed to stand behind her one hundred percent, and she received support form the local AAUP chapter, which declared the episode "another dark blot on the history of academic freedom in Arkansas."

Characteristically, Mom was more concerned about the problems created for Freddy and me than about her own. Meanwhile, Cody and Flipping had taken it upon themselves to look after her interests. Knowing quite a few students at the university, where they planned to enroll the following year, they began making phone calls to organize a support group on the campus. Cody told me my participation in this campaign wasn't wanted, since I would be seized upon too easily as the instigator of any potential student uprising. Cody was convinced he could make the entire thing seem like a groundswell of student emotion, for he believed most of the students, while in sympathy with Mom, were simply unorganized as a voice of protest.

The first indication of exactly how the students felt, and what Cody and his friends had been able to accomplish in just over a week's time, came when one of the legislators who was threatening to file suit appeared on the campus to express his views on the matter. Hundreds of students, many carrying signs both for and against the dismissal, jammed the auditorium, and at least a hundred more stood outside on the lawn. I did not attend myself, but saw plenty of newsreels on the ten o'clock news, and received a first-hand report from Cody later in the night. There had been a lot of shouting and jeering, and also a lot of media attention. On the day following the rally, the head of the economics department informed Mom she was being dismissed immediately. The reasons given did not mention her politics, citing instead such dubious concerns as "a thirty percent disapproval rating on student evaluations." Did this mean seventy percent of the students were being ignored? Another reason given was "failure to participate in departmental improvements," although no specifics were supplied.

Word of the dismissal leaked to the students sometime around noon. By two o'clock there was a massive demonstration in front of the administration building (Cody did nothing to organize this one, he was in gym with me), and the largely symbolic UALR student government was meeting in emergency session to discuss the issue. The demonstration resulted in some good film footage for the television crews, some of which was fed to their affiliated network news centers and nationally aired, but little else. The student government failed to pass a resolution supporting academic freedom, opting instead for a campus-wide referendum the following week to get students' reactions. Meanwhile, the AAUP issued a statement criticizing the university for not consulting the faculty — particularly since faculty opinion was another reason cited for the dismissal. An additional threat by the AAUP to consider blacklisting the university probably frightened no one, since not too long before almost one-fourth of the nation's universities under AAUP censure were located in Arkansas. A professor once was dismissed from Arkansas State Teachers College because of his outspoken opposition to segregation, his use of alcohol and his reputation as a "bohemian." Southern State College of Arkansas once dismissed a professor for "sending Negroes to integrate the church."

Our phone was ringing constantly, until finally none of us could stand it anymore and we unplugged it. I remember at one point that evening, Mom, Freddy, Cody, Mark and I sitting in the living room, slouched against all the available chair and couch space, not saying a word. Mark, who had taken it upon himself to be Freddy's protector at school, shared our exhaustion. When Mom announced she was heading for bed, all eyes followed her out of the room. It was evident she was loved, not only by Freddy and me, but by our two closest friends as well. I was proud of her, proud of Freddy, proud of my friends. And I was tired.

Cody spent the night with me, Mark went home. I hardly remember even looking at Cody when we got into bed, although it was the first time he had stayed over since that strange night when we first went out together. I only remember his mussing my hair while I was sitting on the side of the bed taking my socks off. I slept like death and dreamed all kinds of incredible dreams — Freddy and I playing kick the can back in Wisconsin, Mark and I climbing a mountain in Switzerland, Cody and I passing silver trains at midnight in a sports car. Cody was driving, and as we passed that train, Cody turned the car onto a crossing and all I could see was a blinding light, and hear that clicking beat.

I knew Mom taught one introductory class in economics that was held in a large auditorium and contained just under ninety students. I figured if Cody and I could sneak into *any* class of hers without being noticed, this was the one. Since she was only being allowed to finish out the week before giving up her classes, we both wanted to see her in action as a professor while we had the chance. We waited until Thursday, when she would be delivering her final lecture to the large introductory class, then skipped our own classes and drove over to the university. We had some trouble finding the right auditorium, but made it to the room as the lecture was beginning. Luckily, Mom had her back to the class, so we were able to take seats near the rear without her spotting us. It wasn't that I cared a whole lot if she saw us, but I thought the lecture might come easier for her if she didn't know we were present. I had a feeling she would be giving this last lecture everything she had, and I didn't want her doing anything differently on account of us.

"Class, as you no doubt have heard, today will be my last day as your instructor," she began, standing erect and scanning the room. There was a desk and a rostrum she could have been standing behind, but she stood in the open, appearing both vulnerable and immovable. "I have been accused by many, who have never heard me teach, of instilling in you, my students, socialist ideology rather than an introduction to economic theory. I do not feel I need to defend myself to you, as you have heard me lecture for almost an entire semester and therefore have all the data you need to form your own opinions on the matter. However, today I intend to be guilty of the very thing of which I am accused. I intend to impart to you some of the ideas behind socialism — which is, after all, perhaps the most important school of economic theory to develop in the last one hundred and fifty years. I feel that once you know more about it, you will realize why those in power consider it so dangerous. Ignorance, I believe, is their best friend."

I was studying her voice as much as I studied her words. It wasn't a voice she used with me on any occasion, not when she wished to tell me something important, not when she was angry. This voice was ringing with conviction, concern, and passion. I felt she was truly in her element here, even though she had always seemed a natural at home as well. I wondered for an instant if I had been a disappointment to her, not carrying on in the family tradition of radical politics. She had never pushed me, but did she secretly mourn my continual lack of commitment? Listening to her now was a memory trip through our family photo albums: snapshots of Dad leading protestors through the streets of Milwaukee and Chicago on the coldest of winter days, wrapped in anything they could find that would give them warmth and allow them to deliver their message.

"One of the biggest obstacles to socialism in America over the years has been its upwardly mobile classes. We were taught that anyone in America could pull himself up by his bootstraps, and we developed a system in which respect was assigned to material gains. These new middle classes joined the upper class in looking down on the poor. They followed the upper-class line in demanding that government not interfere in free enterprise. They felt they were somehow better than those who were financially stressed. When welfare programs were established, the upper classes made sure it was the middle classes who paid for them. Two things resulted from this. First, the poor were polarized, with both the middle and upper classes looking down on them. Second, the middle classes, who were having to foot the bill for welfare programs, became increasingly wary of increases in government spending. Their anger was focused on government intervention in their pocketbooks, and on the poor, whom they were being forced to help against their will. What they did not seem to realize was that most of this huge tax burden was going to the military. The amount being spent on important social programs was minuscule by comparison."

Once I dreamed I was sixty — living alone. Didn't have to worry about telling anyone when I came and went. Always knew there would be milk in the fridge. No one to disturb me when I wanted to sleep. Cody appeared in this dream only briefly, with his wife, to invite me to Thanksgiving dinner.

And when I dream I want to evaporate all at once and ascend into nada, *to escape and feel nothing, the bliss of nothing, just for one lifetime to feel nothing, nothing at all.*

Some of us don't feel pleasant living. Some of us don't fit in with society, don't feel at ease anywhere, don't like the daily specials, don't want to buy.

If Cody were my lover would I be happy, I ask myself. I never answer, I only ask, and Cody never answers, never hears me.

Life is so damned sad it's really a shame something had to invent it and not tell us why. What cruelty. Living our lives in a continuous search for meaning in a world without Webster's.

Hard enough looking ahead to working forty hours a week and coming home exhausted, but then to be able to think it all through — just enough comprehension to know how hopeless is the score. What the hell is the point of a brain that defeats you?

"The only way of preserving our natural resources, of keeping our water drinkable and our air breathable, is by strong government regulation of industries to halt pollution. We can no longer allow corporations to wreak havoc on our environment in their insane drives to turn larger profits. Natural resources must be managed carefully if they are to last into the next century.

"American companies are consistently guilty of exploiting other countries' people and resources. Their use and abuse of American workers is made less noticeable, since American workers are not as mistreated as foreigners working under American or European capitalism. I have watched the industry of this country move from north to south because workers were less organized in the South, and easily taken advantage of. Now we are seeing these same companies move their plants to Guatemala and Malaysia, where workers are barely paid enough to survive.

Pure exhaustion. I could certainly feel it in myself, and as I studied my mother, I could see it in the lines of her face. I think: she wears the picture of exhaustion on her face. Her eyes plead passionately for her cause, but her limbs scream exhaustion as they dangle by her torso. She cares deeply, but even her solicitude is assimilated into her exhaustion. There is something almost perfect about her. I study that. I see it as a landscape, painted by some tired, myopic artist who longs to give up his craft, but does not. He waits for someone to take it from him, but is too weak, too ashamed, to take things into his own tired hands. I do not know if I refer to a god. It is a gentle question one would like to have answered. Or perhaps it does not matter. Most things, eventually, seem not to matter. What could it matter to a solar system. But I was accustomed to trivialities unnerving me, so I took this one in stride, hardly even smiling at my own inpercipience, hardly even cursing the limitations inherent in being human.

It is hard to build an image of a creating force any less exhausted than the created, the creatures. If anything, the opposite most likely would be true. I study that. I see it as a burden shared between sympathetic strangers. But already I am reading my own vague hopes into the picture: sympathy. Certainly

there is little material, or even spiritual, evidence upon which to
base such optimistic projections. Surely optimism must be the
most amusing of human follies. I am reminded of the evening
news from a few weeks past: people mutilating pelicans on the
California coast. They had hacked off the birds' upper beaks,
preventing them from catching fish, assuring them of starvation
unless the sympathetic among mankind intervened. Such were
the ways of men ... and probably gods.

It is just as likely human thought is askew to any thought
divine. I have always entertained the hope that human thought
is simply a tangent in a line of "cosmic" thought, with death
erasing the points of limitation for our individual tangents. That
is a pleasant thought, and a splendid cure for exhaustion. It is
easy to see how, if people think point A (birth) and point B
(death) are endpoints of a tangent unlinked with any eternal
cord or line, they become frightened of point B. But if one con-
siders both A and B as merely two in an infinite number of
points on some endless line, as Cody certainly did, then both
points as well as the tangent between them diminish consider-
ably in importance. For some, this may prove too distressing to
consider. For others, and I count myself among their ranks, the
thought that they are currently involved in an altogether in-
significant tangent is indeed the best for which they can hope. It
is, it seems to me, a tangent of pure exhaustion, and once one
has exhausted it, one hopes it is not everything.

"A vast redistribution of wealth is called for, along with a re-
structuring of the political system which will give control of the
government to the people again, instead of to big business interests. It is no longer tolerable for the vast majority of humanity
to work like slaves while a small, elite group hoard the wealth of
the earth, claiming to own the natural resources we all need to
survive.

"The top twenty percent of the U.S. population owns forty
percent of the country's wealth. That seems bad, but not horrible. What *is* horrible is that the top two percent own about

twenty percent of the wealth, while the bottom ten percent has less than 1.5 percent of the nation's wealth to split amongst them.

"Sociologists are keen on measuring the effects poverty has on people living in a wealthy nation. The fact that Houston has had over six hundred murders this year is only one staggering statistic. Something is drastically and desperately wrong with the U.S. system which must be changed. Every year the number of handgun deaths in this country is over *ten thousand*, while countries in Europe have figures ranging between zero and fifty. Why has our society become so violent? Many indicators point to a capitalistic, cut-throat system in which it is instilled in all citizens that they have only themselves to blame for their failures, even though starting out poor in America today is about the same as entering a game of Monopoly after all the property is owned and hotels bought. Our system does not teach sharing, cooperation, or even honesty anymore. It does not, in fact, teach any of the values essential for people to live together peacefully. Through insidious advertising and con-sumer rip-offs, our wealthy classes teach us that lying and cheating are the order of the day. Profit is king, so to hell with the environment, with fair wages, and safe working conditions.

"Our politicians are always screaming so loudly that our land is the land of freedom, yet how many of us are truly free? If, indeed, we enjoy political freedom, of a volatile, frequently endangered sort, what good is this political freedom without economic freedom? We are all excessively manipulated by the wealthy, the corporations, the multinational bandits who have purchased our political system to legitimize their control over all of us."

Only then did she spot me. Our eyes met briefly, she paused just a second in surprise, and I saw a recalcitrant smile curl the corners of her mouth before she continued. Perhaps she was glad for my presence, happy I was sharing this moment.

"How frightened these people must be when even a pro-fessor of economic theory at the University of Arkansas at Little

-118-

Rock must be silenced. I will continue to fight my dismissal in court, but in the meantime, I will miss my job — and I will miss you." She looked over her students one last time. "You may go now," she said, turning her back as if she was going to erase something from the chalkboard, although she had written nothing up there. There was a lengthy hush in the auditorium, then several students began to applaud. Within seconds they were all on their feet, clapping. Ms. Trottingham-Taylor acknowledged their applause by putting one hand on her desk and seeming to teeter momentarily, then raising her head and thanking them with her eyes — tears and all.

Eight

When Christian died, he vomited a pool of blood on both of us as I held his hand. Before this happened, the doctors thought he only had broken his nose. As it turned out, his entire forehead was fractured. A splinter of bone found its way to his brain.

The day began with Flipping, Sarah, Christian, Cody and me taking a trip into the country. Flipping's parents recently had purchased fifteen acres of wooded land at a very good price. They had built a house to their own specifications, put up a fence, and bought several horses. Between work, school, band rehearsals and helping my mother, Flipping also had managed to help his folks build the house. In return they had asked him to invite his friends out some weekend to ride horses. We had packed into Flipping's car around nine a.m. and headed west.

"Wye, Arkansas," Flipping read from the road sign.

"I often ask myself this very question," Christian said. "Why Arkansas?"

"It's not a question, stupid. It's the name of this little town — Wye, Arkansas."

"Do they have A to Z Arkansas?" I asked.

"What county are we in?" Cody wanted to know. Flipping chose to answer Cody's question instead of mine, but I didn't hold it against him.

"We're still in Pulaski."

"Is this place we're going in a dry county?"

"What's it matter? We're all underage anyhow."

"I've got a fake I.D. now," Cody said proudly.

"You don't look twenty-one," Sarah told him.

"It may be in Perry County," Flipping said. "And that's dry as my mouth on Sunday mornings."

"Arkansas sure has a way of making county lines meaningful," Cody moaned.

"Look at that!" Flipping said suddenly. We all looked but saw nothing unusual. "Oh, never mind," he said. "It wasn't what it looked like."

We kept our thoughts to ourselves, except for Christian, who said, "Flipping, you really must learn to think before you speak. I wish you would write that down on your List of Things to Do: I must *think* before I *speak*."

Flipping slowed the car, allowing a chicken to get safely off the road. "If anyone makes a joke about this one, I'll bean him," he threatened.

"Well, I'm not a him," Sarah said. "How do chickens perpetuate themselves?"

Silence.

"They egg each other on."

More silence.

"I can't believe my parents live in a place called Natural Steps."

"Arkansas has some very strange names for their towns," I agreed.

"Like Bald Knob and Tomato."

"Ratio and Fifty Six."

"Oil Trough and Marked Tree."

"There's a Flippen, Arkansas, too."

"And a Cody and a Washington," Cody added.

"Every state has a Washington," Sarah informed him.

"My favorite's Goobertown."

"Yeah, remember that night we were listening to state basketball scores and the sportscaster said 'Hooker beat Goobertown'?"

"What a riot! I bet Goobertown's always getting beat."

"I bet they *enjoy* getting beat!"

"Would you all please shut up!" Sarah insisted.

"Did you know a former governor of Texas once appointed a man who had been dead for two years to serve on the State Health Commission?" I asked, just to change the subject.

"Seems like that would make him unqualified somehow."

"Actually, there are two Hookers in Arkansas," said Cody.

"Really?"

"Yeah, there's one up around Pigott, and another south of Pine Bluff near Lake Dick."

"I *said* shut up," Sarah warned.

"We have arrived!" Flipping announced. "This is Natural Steps."

No sooner had we piled out of the car than Flipping's father was yelling at us from across a field, waving us toward him. It didn't take long to climb over the wooden fence separating us and run to meet him. Having never met the man, I was a bit surprised to see his hair was almost as long as his son's.

"Hi," he said, trying to encompass everyone in his welcoming glance. His eyes settled, ultimately, on Flipping. "That old mare done had a colt and I can't find it nowheres. I've already looked down in the south corner and around the stables. It's prob'ly somewheres down in them woods over the hill. If we spread out we could prob'ly find it pretty quick."

"I didn't know that mare was pregnant," Flipping said.

Mr. Benning allowed himself a small laugh. "Hnn-hnn! Truth is, neither did I till last week. Had t'ave happened 'fore I bought 'er."

"How long does it take a horse—"

"Oh, 'bout 'leven months."

"Have any idea what the father might've looked like?"

"No, I bought her from Old Man Watkins over in Bland, but I din't think he had a stallion on the place. I hadn't really planned on breeding her, just wanted her for Timmy to ride."

Timmy, Flipping's younger cousin, had been raised by the Bennings since his parents were confined in Cummins Prison. Cody had mentioned them once or twice; they had been arrested for growing marijuana on their farm, and had been in prison for most of Timmy's life. Having watched Timmy grow up, Flipping pretty much thought of him as a brother.

We split into pairs, Flipping going with his father in one direction, Sarah with Christian in another, and Cody with me in a third. Passing some wild muscadines, Cody and I made a mental note to come back and pick them later when we weren't busy. Cody was disappointed I knew what they were, but my mother already had discovered them and made jelly from some she gathered the day we went to get firewood. We also had sampled muscadine wine one evening, which was a truly weird experience, muscadines being the bastard Southern cousin of the grape family, and tasting, as their name would indicate, rather musky.

We passed by a stock pond, or at least I assumed it was a stock pond. I stopped for a minute to skip a rock across it. The water was so still the stone skipped ten times, then landed on the far shore.

"I imagine that's a blue hole," Cody said.

He had me this time. "What's a blue hole?" I inquired, knowing he would be pleased I had to ask.

"I imagine you're looking at one," he said.

I didn't say anything, just looked at him as if I might.

"A blue hole is a bottomless pit. Bauxite is a very big thing around here, you know, and they used to dig these enormous holes, then just leave them or fill them up with water when they moved to another site. I doubt if they still do that, but in any case, all over central Arkansas you see ponds like this. They look like a normal stock pond, but if you happened to drown in one, you would just keep on sinking. No telling how deep that thing might be."

"Hey, we found him!"

I recognized the voice as Christian's. That figured, somehow. Cody and I ran in the direction of the voice. When we got to Christian and Sarah, we saw the colt, and also a nervous black horse in an ill temper, standing between us and the colt.

"That doesn't look like a horse that just had a colt," Sarah said.

Cody took a look underneath. "Can't be. That's a gelding."

"What's it doing with the colt?"

"Good question."

Flipping came tromping over the hill. "Shiloh! Get away! Go on now! Git!"

Shiloh would not hear of it.

"Where's your father?" Christian asked.

"He'll be here. Soon as he saw Shiloh he went back to get a bucket of feed in case we need it."

"What does that horse think it's doing?"

"How should I know? Horses are incredibly dumb."

"Not as dumb as cats," Cody said.

Sarah and Christian usually took offense whenever Cody slandered cats, but this time they said nothing. Flipping, meanwhile, was trying to pry his way between Shiloh and the colt. Shiloh did not like it in the least, but because he had too many humans to keep an eye on, Flipping was able to get close enough to touch the colt.

"It's a male," he told us.

"That means a blue halter."

"Christian, you can be so annoying."

Flipping's father came back with a bucket of grain. He gradually coaxed Shiloh toward the stable, answering questions about when the colt was born and how it was separated from its mother. At the stable he put the colt into a stall with the mother, which produced several conniption fits from Shiloh.

"Why is Shiloh trying to mother that colt?" Flipping asked. I think we had all been wanting to ask this question, but were afraid we'd get the same answer Flipping got:

Hell if I know. That horse ain't got a lick a' sense."

The mother did not act particularly thrilled to see her off-spring. The colt was looking everywhere for a place to suck, but the mare was moving around within the limits of the stall, making it very difficult. I'm sure all of us laughing at her ineptitude as a mother didn't help her nerves, but eventually she resigned herself to her maternal role. Once we had our fill of the horses, Flipping took us to a recently harrowed field and taught us how to drive his father's tractor. Then Christian, Flipping and Sarah saddled the three best riding horses on the place, while Cody and I combed the fields for muscadines.

We could not forego the temptation of stripping bare the first blackberry patch we encountered. The second patch was also devoured, then, quite unexpectedly, we came across a maze of tangled vines and thorns, overflowing with huge blackberries the likes of which made those we had already consumed seem hardly edible. By this time Sarah, Christian and Flipping had found us, dismounted from their horses, and joined us in stuffing ourselves.

I noticed Sarah had berry stains all over her hands and face, as did we all, but Sarah had them all over her clothes as well. She had obviously been enjoying herself. I decided a few more stains would hurt nothing, so I gathered up a handful of overly-ripe berries and flung them at her. She let forth with such a blood-curdling scream I was afraid I might have killed her somehow. But as I stood there in bewildered concern, she attacked me. She had me down in a moment and was smearing berries in my face and hair. Once recovered, I freed myself only through fierce, competitive struggle. Then I began a second attack, but quickly was put on the defensive again by a barrage from Sarah's amazingly accurate arm. Everyone watched us for a while, then Christian and Cody began throwing berries indiscriminately at both Sarah and me, as Sarah was the first to realize. She made the mistake of pausing long enough for me to catch her full in the face with several berries, but decided to forgive me in favor of playing a new game.

"Look at them!" she yelled. In the excitement, I had been

oblivious to the attacks coming from the side. Now that Sarah dilated the scope of my attention, we became even more excited than before. I was ready to emit some wild battle cry when Christian and Cody clobbered me from both sides. I was actually *wet* from berries, looking more purple than white, as Sarah and I defended ourselves from the new attackers. Flipping, momentarily caught in the cross-fire, managed to escape without serious staining. Sarah, meanwhile, had seen Cody's open shirt as an obvious target and whammied several bull's-eyes onto his chest. Cody ran behind a bush to plan some type of strategy. Christian and I appeared evenly matched, which is to say we both were suffering considerably. With Cody temporarily out of view, Sarah came to my aid and together we gave Christian a thorough bathing in berry juice. Unexpectedly, Cody leapt from behind us. Sarah screamed, as she was unarmed, but I met Cody's attack with a handful of berries to the face. We somehow managed to trip each other, Cody cursing as he fell into a patch of stickers. Christian and Sarah circled each other until Sarah abruptly decided she was tired of the whole mess, got back on her horse, and took off up the hill. Christian followed her, after wasting his last handful of berries on a terribly bad shot.

"You sure are going to look a sight at the dinner table," Flipping told us, before riding off to join the others. The sudden realization that we need be presentable later in the evening put a damper on our fun. The only thing left to do was fall on the ground laughing, studying our injuries. Cody rolled over next to me, smiling widely, put his arm around me, smeared berries into my face, and ran away. I chased him, caught him without too much difficulty, then hauled him down and sat on him. He kept pointing to my face and laughing hysterically, so I sat on his hands, too. At first he struggled, then he quit and just lay there grinning at me. We were behind the bushes where nobody could see us. The berry-stained smiles we gave each other were so filled with love, it was all I could do to bridle my passion. Then I noticed that we *were* being watched, by some kid on a bicycle who looked to be about nine or ten. I assumed this must be Timmy, and found I was right once Cody, following my eyes, sprang to his feet and yelled "Timmy!" in greeting. It reminded me of the time Cody's boss had surprised us at the service station. Seemed like we couldn't jump on each other without someone coming 'round.

"You look a mess," Timmy said to Cody.

Cody made like he would go for him, so Timmy took off on his bike and didn't stop until he was up near the house. Cody and I then walked down to the pond and washed ourselves off a bit.

No one asked if I'd ever ridden a horse before, but in fact I had. My only regret once Cody and I got our chance was seeing him hop on the palomino I'd wanted to ride myself. Instead, I rode a dark, gangly stallion, consoled that at least the four of us had color-coordinated hair. We stayed close together, at first, with Cody pointing out the several native oaks on the Benning property. They were obvious enough, having about four times the circumference of the other trees. Cody explained how once they covered the entire countryside, blocking the sun, making it possible for the early settlers to ride long distances without getting tangled in undergrowth. I had wondered about this, imagining the pioneers, and the Indians before them, carrying machetes everywhere to clear paths.

Just across the fence at the northern end of the Benning property was a cemetery, very old and small, which obviously attracted few, if any, visitors. Cody and I dismounted, tied the horses to a fence post, then had a look at some of the tombstones, of which only a few were legible. It seemed most of these people had come from one of four families — West, Reed, Greer or Steed — and a great many of them had died in 1882 within a month of each other. I wondered if anyone was alive who would know what caused their deaths.

Back on the horses, we split up without discussing it. I started riding in one direction, Cody another, and neither changed course to join the other. For my part, I explored the western edge of the property with no great interest, wondering what Cody was doing, and wishing he wasn't always on my mind. When I noticed it was getting late, I headed back to the house, finding Cody had beat me there and was washing up at the pump in the backyard. I took the horse to the stable to unsaddle and curry.

Mr. Benning and Timmy were there, still examining the new colt. As I was brushing the horse I heard the most awful howling sound coming from somewhere in the distance.

"What was that?" I asked.

Mr. Benning laughed his little laugh again. "Hnn-hnn! Truth is, we don't know. I ain't never heard nothing like it, and I don't know what it is."

"It sounds like it's half-bird, half-human, half-dog," I ventured.

"That's three halves," Timmy said.

"Never mind him, he's studying fractions."

But I minded him anyway and said to Timmy, "Well, it *sounds* like a creature and a half."

"Hnn-hnn!" said Mr. Benning. "If you feel up to it, we might go have ourselves a look after we eat and see if'n we can spot it."

"No thanks," I said. "We'd probably find something half-bird, half-human and half-dog."

Inside the house, Mrs. Benning was trying to get everyone situated for dinner. She had met me at the door with a cheese grater under her arm, wringing her hands with a dishtowel, and wearing a red-and-white checkered tent dress which reminded me of a Purina dog food bag. "Pleased to meet ya," she'd said, offering a freshly-toweled hand, then hurrying back into the kitchen. The lighting in the house was incredibly bright, but Flipping had warned us beforehand of his mother using two 100-watt bulbs in each overhead light fixture. It was a clean, well-lighted place, and we prepared to partake of our daily *nada*.

"Timmy! You git that blasted turtle out of this kitchen right now!"

"It ain't a turtle, it's a terrapin."

"Hell, child, they're all turtles to me, now git 'em out!"

The conversation over dinner had at first centered around slugs and eels. It began with Timmy proclaiming, "The last thing I'd ever want to eat would be an eel." Mr. Benning was quick to agree, then changed his mind, saying he'd rather eat an eel than a slug. Then they began to argue over which was worse — an argument which ended some five minutes later when Mrs. Benning dropped both her hands to the table and said, "I *swear*, if I hear one more word about an eel or a slug, you'll both be eatin' 'em for lunch tomorrow!"

So instead Timmy and Mr. Benning began to argue over what they'd watch on television after dinner. Timmy wanted to see some movie I'd never heard of, while Mr. Benning favored a football game.

"You jist wanna see that movie 'cause you're interested in the girls."

"Not yet I'm not," Timmy retorted.

Mrs. Benning asked if the food was all right.

"These scalloped potatoes could use some salt and pepper," Flipping answered.

"Did I forget to set the shakers on the table? Well, you know where they are if you want 'em."

"They don't need it that bad."

Mrs. Benning threw her napkin down on her plate. "Too lazy to git the salt and pepper! People used ta go all the ways ta India ta git it, and you won't even go ta the kitchen cab'nets!" Then she dropped her voice and asked if anyone else needed the salt or pepper.

She was already up to get them, but Cody, Christian, Sarah and I each exclaimed that everything was fine. The food was incredibly good — an opinion the four of us tried to express all at once, unfortunately.

As I brushed the hair from my eyes, a loose one fell onto my enchiladas. One was a cheese enchilada and the other had something to do with meat. These were Mrs. Benning's specialties, not so much because they tasted any better than the other dishes, but because she had figured out how to make them herself, without a recipe or her mother to guide her — at least that's what she told us. I suspected the meat enchilada was venison.

"You know old Mrs. Potts?" Mrs. Benning was saying to Flipping on her return with the salt and pepper shakers.

"I know her son," Flipping said.

"Oh yes, I remember him too. A little twirp, he was. Went ta Oral Roberts University, didn't he? Anyway, what I was sayin' was, Mrs. Potts just got outta Baptist Hospital yesterday, and she called 'while ago."

"What was wrong with her?"

"She had ta have an operation on her hemorrhoids."

I noted for future reference that eels and slugs were not suitable conversation at Mrs. Benning's table, but hemorrhoids were.

"Well, that's pretty rough on a old woman when 'er kids git borned again," Mr. Benning said from behind his glass of tea.

Christian and Flipping cracked up immediately, and Timmy, grasping something funny had been said, began laughing with his mouth open, adding vegetables to Flipping's plate.

Mrs. Benning did not seem to think it was very funny, but after a short silence she continued to dominate the conversation, as everyone else seemed more interested in eating than talking. She had some strange expressions, and it seemed her favorite word was "stinky." She told Timmy to take off his "stinky cap," and told Sarah how boys were "just the stinkiest things I ever saw." She also was extremely animated. When she asked Flipping to take a meatloaf to his grandmother once he got back into town, and Flipping replied by asking if his grandma had got too feeble to cook, Mrs. Benning whirled around in surprise, both her knife and fork sticking straight up in the air.

"Why! She's nothing of the sort! The auxiliary is meetin' tomorrow — having a potluck in fact — and she was ta bring some sort of meat dish. I promised her I'd make it so she could git those begonias planted Miss Sutton give her."

"I bet they smell like mothballs," Timmy interrupted.

"You hush," Mrs. Benning scolded. "Old Miss Sutton hant smelt like mothballs in years."

At this suggestion both Flipping and Timmy protested loudly.

"Why, I passed her on the street about a month ago when I went to see Grandma, and she smelt just like a mothball!"

"I mowed her lawn last week and her whole house, her whole yard smelt like mothballs. I bet she uses them for fertilizer. Those begonias she gave Grandma are gonna smell up the whole place, you just wait and see!"

"Okay. *Okaay!*" Mrs. Benning surrendered, hands raised higher in the air.

"There were always two things I tried to impress upon Flipping," she said, with a perfectly straight face. "Never assume anything, and don't be overly cautious."

All around the table people sat with their forks in mid-air, staring either at her or Flipping, pondering this wisdom. I thought I could feel the breeze from Sarah's head spinning.

Mrs. Benning continued, seriously, but also somewhat cheerfully, "You know, I've never seen the point in worrying the young about their future, when with all the bombs and kooks running around these days, they might not even have one."

Instead, she decided to worry Flipping about his past and present.

"Have you been goin' to bed at a decent hour?"

"All God's hours are decent, Mother."

"Well if the Good Lord wanted us ta be stayin' up all night, he woulda given us eyes what would see in the dark."

Mr. Benning bravely came to his son's defense. "Honey, he gave you those goddamn hunerd-watt bulbs, so stop your yelping."

"And *you* quit being so cantankerous!"

"I'm not being cantankerous, I was just telling—"

"Why, you *are so!* You're so ornery if a tube a' ketchup said 'tear here,' you'd go and tear it way over there!"

I tried to imagine growing up with this woman as my mother, but the vision would never gel. On the other hand, I couldn't imagine having Mr. Benning for a father, either. Flipping already had told us his father had a vendetta against adages. He would sit around for hours trying to teach their fifteen-year-old Labrador tricks, and every time he made instant coffee he would stand before the stove watching the pot until the water boiled.

There's the time which would not tell.

He also claimed he held no grudge against anyone, and had written several letters to state prosecutors asking them to amend their spiels to "The people of the State of Arkansas, *except* Mr. Avery F. Benning, versus so-and-so." As far as Flipping knew, he had never received a reply. Now, he invited us all into the den for some after-dinner hash, seeming genuinely surprised and disappointed that Sarah and I did not smoke the stuff.

There's the woman whose place was in the car wash.

Cody allowed himself a hit or two on this occasion, possibly just for politeness' sake.

There's the game Seattle lost because Mrs. Patrick of Walla Walla did not close her eyes on fourth and twenty.

As we were about to leave, Mr. Benning followed us out, searching for his dog.

"Just whistle for 'em," Timmy said, "he'll come."

"*You* whistle for 'em."

"I don't know how to whistle."

"Well you ain't gonna git me to whistle. I'm afeared somethin' might come a chargin' outta them woods what was half-bird, half-human and half-dog."

There's the student who went home to Gallup, finding everything exactly the same.

It was agreed Timmy would go back into town to spend the night with Flipping, and Mr. Benning would pick him up Sunday night since he needed to drive into town anyway. Although I couldn't imagine what there was at the Loft which would be entertaining to a ten-year-old, except perhaps the dead butter-flies on the walls, Timmy was very excited about spending the night with Flipping.

Riding home, Sarah entertained us with jokes, seemingly oblivious to a child in the car. I suppose if Timmy lived with a man who smoked hash and a woman who was entirely capable of brainwarp, we needn't have worried about being a good influence. Sarah certainly did not.

"You see, there was this salesman, and he goes up to this house out in the country, knocks on the door, and a little boy answers. So the salesman asks the kid if his mother's at home, and the kid says, 'Naw, she's over in the field making out with the sheep.' Of course the salesman is startled, so once he gets his breath back he asks the boy, 'Well, doesn't that bother you?' And the little boy says, 'Naaaaaaaa.'"

There's Mick Jagger, encrusted with a small, leafy bryo-phytic plant with tufted stems bearing sex organs at the tips.

Flipping was driving along at a good clip, perhaps just over the speed limit. The night was clear, the stars were out. The radio played a salute to Motown soul. One of my favorite songs by the Jackson Five, "Don't Know Why I Love You," was play-ing at a nice, heady volume, and I was feeling fine. It had been a good day. Flipping's folks, despite their eccentricities, were good people.

Christian and Timmy were riding in the front seat with Flipping. For some reason I had been made to sit in the middle of the rear seat between Cody and Sarah. When Flipping topped the next hill, I happened to be looking straight ahead, so I immediately saw the car coming toward us, in our lane, without its lights on. Flipping, seeing it at the same time, assaulted his brakes with urgency. I performed two minutes of mental activ-ity in less than two seconds: wondering if we had time to swerve and miss the car, knowing we did not; wondering if the force of the impact would be strong enough to kill us. I knew we were about to be hurt, and chances were some of us would be hurt badly. I heard Flipping say, "Oh fuck," to himself and to all of us, to all the little "g" gods who might be listening, might be watching, placing their bets. And then the cars collided, and then all was still. During the critical moment of impact I know only what happened to myself. I plowed into the back of the front seat, a buffer which apparently saved me, for I didn't feel injured. The impact of all three of us slamming into the back of the front seat tore it from the floorboard.

There's the snowflake which fell in Duluth in 1958 which was exactly like the one which fell in Basil in 1752.

I heard someone outside the car murmuring, "Jesus, Jesus," then saying he would go call an ambulance. Sarah was still, lying in the floor of the car, clutching her neck, breathing but not moving. I looked at Cody, who looked at me, then we both looked over the top of the front seat.

Cody opened his door and went around to the back of the car and threw up. I felt like doing the same, but didn't. I tried to focus on something important, and what I found to attend to was Christian, for he seemed to need it the most. He was bleeding from the nose, where he had hit the dashboard, and he said he couldn't see. Flipping had been wearing a seat belt, as always, and didn't seem hurt. Timmy, coming out from under the dash where he'd been thrown, seemed to be okay, although he was rubbing his head. Sarah was still on the floor of the back seat. Fearing she might have whiplash, she didn't want to move until an ambulance arrived.

It didn't take them long to get there. Christian was put in one and Sarah in the other. A policeman got in the ambulance with Christian. After consultation with Cody, it was agreed he would go to the hospital with Sarah and I would ride with Christian. Flipping had to stay behind to talk to the police.

The cop riding with Christian and me seemed to be along just to make obviously irrelevant racist remarks. The ambulance driver and paramedics tried to ignore him, but I could tell he was upsetting Christian. At the hospital, the cop repeatedly referred to Christian as "girl," presumably because of his long hair. A nurse finally asked the cop to leave, then called me over and asked if I had any marijuana, looking doubtful when I answered "no."

"Look, I'm trying to help," she said. "I know that policeman's going to search you sooner or later, so if you have any pot on you, give it to me and I'll hide it."

Casually, I walked over to Christian, who was lying on a high, narrow bed, and removed the lid I knew was inside his jeans. Christian didn't open his eyes, which looked as if they were beginning to swell shut, but when he felt my hand inside his pants he grabbed my arm. Just by touching me he knew who I was and said my name. The nurse walked behind me and opened an opaque plastic bag, into which I dropped Christian's lid. She then walked quickly away, while Christian continued to grasp my arm.

"Stay with me, Trotsky," he said.

I took his hand and put my other hand on his forehead, which felt as cold as ice. With a start, Christian sat up and began to vomit blood all over himself and all over me. And then he died.

There's the bolt of lightning which knocked Farmer Matthews off his tractor, then struck him again, just to make sure he was dead.

Nine

Everywhere, there was the dagger of memory: the Loft, one night when I was alone with Christian and we got off on the subject of our "Most Embarrassing Moments." We both had some real winners, but I suppose just about everyone does.

"I have these little snapshots of my most horrible moments that I carry around in my subconscious at all times," Christian said. "And then some night when I'm at my most depressed, when I honestly don't think I can stand another minute of this old world, these little snapshots of horror will suddenly appear in my mind one after another, and I'll think about what a shit I was ten years ago, something I did that I'm really ashamed of."

I knew exactly what he meant. I had those same snapshots, and they appeared at the most inappropriate times to haunt me. They were so embarrassingly personal I had thought I might be one of the only people who experienced them with such pain. Christian, in his casual way, proved me wrong.

Cody attended the funeral with my Mom and me, Flipping with his own family. Sarah was in the hospital with a broken neck. In many ways I would rather have stayed away myself. The minister made insulting presumptions ("Christian was a firm believer in God's love"), the music was morose.

Like Flipping, Christian had been an only child. His parents, whom I'd never met, looked completely destroyed. One good look told you this was a couple who had given up on life long ago. It appeared life made them nervous; I could easily feature them staying shut up in their house, in their car, or in offices or in front of the television. I felt for them, wondering what such a tragedy could mean to people already living in fear of the world. Christian's mother stared at the floor throughout the service, her hands pulled tight between her knees, her shoulders slouched downward as if she wanted to make herself disappear. Christian's father nervously looked around, seemingly puzzled by the strangers who had come to pay tribute to his son.

Riding in the procession after the service, the sun came into our car at such an angle as to cast across Cody's face a reflection of a translucent rainbow Freddy had stuck onto a corner of the front windshield. The reflection hit Cody neatly across the cheek. From the back seat, I stared at Cody's cheek most of the way to the cemetery, until a change in direction removed the rainbow.

Roads surrounded the cemetery on two sides, with railway track on another, while on the fourth side it had begun to spill over into an open field. It was here Christian was buried. A train approached as his coffin was lowered into the ground, reminding me of Cody's vignette. *DEATH: Passing silver trains at midnight in a sports car.* I wondered if Cody was thinking the same, fairly certain he was. But this train, Missouri Pacific blue, was from the look of it not a properly constructed train, for most of the empty cars had been placed directly behind the engine, with the loaded cars at the end. This meant that if the train should have to brake suddenly, there would be a high risk of the cars in the middle waffling, causing the train to derail. I was quite willing to consider this possibility, to mentally chastise the railway engineers for not following the proper rules of safety, to think of *anything at all* except the matter at hand.

Before leaving the cemetery, Cody introduced me to Red Stanley. I recognized him from school, one among hundreds of students I saw now and then but did not know. Red was much better looking than the persistently negative comments about him had led me to imagine. At least now I could give Mark credit for better taste. Red and I had nothing to say, despite our connections through Christian and Flipping, and more recently through Mark. After Cody spoke to him for a minute, we left for my house.

At home, Mom's dismissal continued to have its repercussions. We still had to keep the phone off the hook to maintain any privacy; we also had two baskets of unopened mail on top of the washer and dryer. Since nine out of ten letters were what you might call hate mail, we weren't sure what to do with them, not wanting to throw away unread those few letters of support mixed in with the others. Among the many people beginning to view us with hostility was our postman.

Mark was at our house, keeping Freddy company. Mom discovered we were out of coffee and asked if I would mind going after some. Before I could answer, Mark volunteered to go on his bike. The idea of riding a bike appealed to me at the moment, so I borrowed Freddy's and we took off for the store.

"What kind of coffee do you like?" I asked Mark.

"Prime Choice," he said.

"That's a dog food," I told him.

"Well, it's Prime *something.*"

"A prime example of your stupidity," I teased. To make sure he knew I was kidding, I smiled widely and rode up beside him, trying to muss his hair. He wheeled away from me, happy to have a grudge.

"You probably mean Taster's Choice," I said. "But that's instant coffee and I'm sure Mom wants ground."

I bought a can of something I had seen in our kitchen before, then I decided to grind some myself, choosing a Peruvian blend. Not expecting it to cost as much as it did, I had to borrow a quarter from Mark to help pay the tab. I put the sack in my jacket and zipped it up tight for the ride home. The smell of the freshly-ground coffee circulated up through the neck as I rode in the chilly wind, surrounding and caressing me with the soothing aroma of coffee beans.

When we walked into the house, Cody asked if I'd like to go for a drink.

"Sure," I said, "but I'm totally broke."

"I don't want either of you driving if you're going to be drinking," Mom called from the kitchen. In light of recent events, we weren't going to argue. Cody said he thought he'd go over to the bar anyway, and his sister could give him a ride home later. He didn't think she would mind giving me a ride home also, and he was willing as always to buy my drinks, but I declined the offer. Mark left soon after Cody, and Mom retired to her bedroom to study legal documents and look over her fan mail. Freddy asked if I felt like playing hockey, but I couldn't deal with that. Instead, I tried writing some poetry, scratching through or tearing up everything I wrote except:

> Oh do a fallen friend dance
> and show me your empty pockets.
> What was that in your eyes what
> banged away at my empty sockets?

With Mom and Freddy long ago in bed, I sat in the den by the dwindling fire, not wanting to listen to music or anything else, feeling it would all sound like so much bullshit compared to the aching sadness in the core of what was me. I watched a small moth flutter up and extinguish itself in the light of the table lamp, but I did not find a lesson in that. I had drunk two cups of coffee and was not expecting to sleep. Then I heard a tapping at our front door. At three a.m. the door could only scream disaster or Cody. I felt prepared for either as I opened it, and Cody immediately grabbed hold of my shoulders and looked into my eyes. I could see his eyes were bloodshot, and it was impossible not to notice the alcohol on his breath. I had never seen him looking so badly. The sparkle in his eyes was missing and he wasn't carrying himself well, looking instead as if his body were trying to cave in on itself. It occurred to me he had changed shirts since I'd last seen him, and was now wearing the one I'd given him that first time he slept over. Cody handed me a slip of paper, then let me go. I read this:

> Standing back, frost full of Decembers.
> Breaths blown, transfixed upon the cabin window.
> I can dream to remember.
> And memory serves to transcend
> the loneliness of vacant moments
> without the diamond back company
> of a good friend.

So he had spent his evening the same as I, even writing on a similar theme. Telling him I liked his better than my own, I showed Cody what I'd written. After reading it he simply looked at me and said, "All bodhisattvas either write or paint."

I thought about this while Cody went to the bathroom. While the nebulous level of many conversations with Cody intrigued me, it was also a bit of an annoyance since he could so easily deploy abstraction to his own advantage. Of all his theories, his insistence that everything happened through cause and effect was the one I thought most plausible. It was even hard to dispute, although I couldn't help wondering how he would have applied it to the death of our friend. What cause had effected Christian's death? And what effect would his death have other than to sadden his friends? What was the purpose of the Christians in one's life? For what reasons do paths cross?

In my room, Cody stumbled through the steps of undressing as I spread the covers about on the bed. Completely nude, he fell forward onto the bed, not bothering with the cover. I began to do all those things one does when putting away one's house for the night, all the while thinking of Cody lying face down on my bed. Although I knew I'd never do anything which might jeopardize our friendship, I was struck by the strength of the temptation. I stood by the bed, not knowing if he was asleep or if he sensed I was staring at him. The bright, overhead light was on. I switched it off.

I lay awake in bed, wondering if I dared to touch him,

finally deciding it was a bad idea. With lions and humans, you can't be too careful. Just as I was about to turn and face the other direction, Cody moved over and wrapped his body around mine, resting his head on my shoulder. Neither of us said a word, and before long I knew he'd fallen asleep. I wondered if other boys had felt his warmth in their beds. I doubted it somehow, and that made the experience all the nicer. Wrapped in his arms, I thought of many things, but mostly of Christian. For the first time, the thought struck home that we wouldn't be seeing him again. A tear rolled down my cheek, seemingly dancing to Cody's heartbeat, and fell on his shoulder: the shoulders that carried Cody through his life with a sense of independence, until a night like tonight, when he would melt on you. I kissed his sleeping head, so full of dreams. Eventually my own desire for sleep surpassed my desire to stay awake and feel Cody holding me, although I would liked to have felt him wrapped around me forever.

In the following weeks, the chairman of the UALR economics department issued a prepared statement defending the reasons for firing Mom. Once again Cody involved himself with organizing support for her on campus, while Mom met with her lawyers to plan a suit against the university. While Mom was convinced she could prove her dismissal was for political reasons, the administration continued to insist it was a result of her poor teaching record. In the chairman's statement, he mentioned two surveys of student opinion regarding the competence of Ms. Taylor as a teacher. Although he claimed the survey results were in the economic department's files, the campus newspapers were denied access and could find no evidence the surveys were ever conducted. The chairman said Ms. Taylor's grading procedures, failure to make sufficient use of the required texts, and other "patterns of incompetence" led to the dismissal. Meanwhile, the UALR student government released the results of their student poll. Voicing their opinion on the question, "Should Ms. Helen Trottingham-Taylor be allowed to continue teaching at UALR?" students responded "yes" by a vote of 627 to 419. Hardly overwhelming support, but at least the evidence wasn't being kept hidden in a departmental file.

The department chairman's only comment on the student vote was, "You can look at it and say that a significant minority — forty percent — objected to Ms. Taylor."

Since the accident, several little nervous tics had crept into my life. For instance, I was forever investigating my zipper, even though it was always zipped up when I inspected it. In bed at night I would check the clock five or six times to make sure I had set the alarm, even though I knew I had. My watch was constantly wound to the limit. I had also become something of a nervous wreck over my lack of sleep, and was going to bed at early hours hoping I would accidentally drift off, although, of course, I never did.

"Seven o'clock's gonna come mighty early," I said to Freddy one night as I went to bed at ten.

"Not before seven, I hope," Freddy responded. He helped to keep me sane that way. Observing my peculiar behavior, he intuitively knew his best reaction was to be himself even more than usual.

Cody and I were spending many a night at the Magic Theatre and several other bars Cody could charm our way into, drinking ourselves into a near stupor, writing in notebooks, not saying much. Like Pavlov's dog salivating at the ring of the bell, I had drunk so many screwdrivers I could get a buzz on my morning orange juice.

Cody, when inebriated, frequently thought everything in the universe was falling into place quite nicely. Each acquaintance he ran into — and Cody ran into people he knew everywhere, everyday — was a cause for celebration. He *knew* he would see them, it was destiny. And the conversation would be immediately important, although the other person might not grasp the importance, or even the topic. Cody would spend several intense minutes with them, then perhaps suggest they have a drink, or he might simply leave them and become engaged with some other person until this one, too, bored him. Nevertheless, the intoxicated Cody seemed perpetually amazed by people and the world. Drunk or not, he could be so disarmingly honest, so brazenly sincere and intelligent in his diligent pilgrimage, I couldn't help wonder if eventually he'd drive himself crazy through his own longing.

So many evenings and early mornings I passed with Cody in bars and in between bars, sometimes enjoying his company, frequently walking dazed through city streets trying to sort through my latest barrage of emotions, often the partisan observer to Cody's confrontations with friends. I saw it happen time and again: those moments in the night when energy flies through the darkness from soul to soul, one minute transmitting from one to the other, the next moment racing both ways at once, a second later a linkage of electric fusion collapsing in space as their bodies touch, embrace. I stand smiling as the energy, illusive as will-o-the-wisp, dissipates, severs, and a static hum of Cody reaches out to me to carry him to the next encounter.

You can hug an image until it bursts apart, you can tie a friend in knots around your heart in hopes he'll stop the bleeding. Sometimes I felt helpless, for I could feel the same claws which tore at Cody's gut, and I could hear him at his wit's end, screaming out to me. A razor's edge on chalkboard scream, the "save me" kind little kids use when the dog's too big and doesn't smile. This was the terror which drove us through the night, until Cody was so tired I'd find him leaning against an alley wall to pee. I'd be waiting on a corner, clearing my throat to the air, staring at the little trace of blood, a red stream of consciousness, in my spit, left on the sidewalk — Kilroy was here.

Finally, in the early hours of the morning, we'd find the only restaurant open till five a.m., which was run by a transplanted Italian and specialized in seafood and pizza. On the menu were a number of unlikely cephalopod entrees such as squid tofu and "octopus served up in its own ink," which always seemed to me the way one should serve up William F. Buckley, Jr. or Patrick Buchanan. Cody and I would frequently spend more than an hour in the restaurant scribbling bits of insanity into our notebooks.

> *When we dissolve into a spasm of thought, we perceive*
> *the concrete art of expression — Hesse's glass beads.*
> *Even Sweet Emily sent them out to be seen.*

Often our choice from the menu was something called Capricious Pizza, which was topped with "Depending on the humor of the cook." Our cook was frequently in a black olive, green pepper, pineapple and tuna humor, but we'd eat it anyway, and we would write and not say much, and finally we'd ask our waiter if we could pay. To our amusement, he'd say we could, but we never gave up hope of him someday exclaiming, "No! Certainly not!"

I was kept broke by these excursions, for I preferred being broke to having Cody forever paying my way, which he'd have done without hesitation. Sometimes we'd check the *Gazette's* "listings," but there was rarely anything of interest in town, and I often felt the listings were important not so much for providing us with things to do as with excuses to get together. It might begin with: "Ya wanna go see this production of *Tartuffe* at the university?"

"Sure, but let's go have a drink first."

And before we knew it, we'd have completely forgotten *Tartuffe*, as we enjoyed our evening together, an evening related to others as, "Well, we'd started out to see *Tartuffe*..."

"Oh yeah, I meant to see that."

"...but we had a few drinks and never made it."

Pity the poor performing arts.

Often I would return home drunk in the tender dawn and steal Mark from Freddy's room, careful not to wake up Freddy. Mark did not mind these intrusions on his sleep, for they pro-

vided us one of the few opportunities we had to be in bed together. As the sun was rising, we would be falling, into bed and
arms, flesh touching flesh in something like passion, something
like comfort. Sex, sure. Sex put the mind at ease just thinking,
yes, I had this friend, this incredible young friend who was willing to let me touch his body in every way I desired, to explore
his flesh and discover new ways of loving him. I was always
struck by this beauty, this mad, sincere beauty in my bed, who
wasn't in some other bed, who was loving me. There was often
something like white-out, I think because it was frequently
dawning when we made our love. I always thought of photos
developing in the darkroom, of an image slowly appearing in
white space, of southwestern Wisconsin during the Pleistocene
Epoch, those icebergs resting against her side, waiting for a land
to grow: Mark and I embracing recklessly in geophysical
romance. It never felt complete, and it often came off badly; but
give me the next night and three drinks and I was ready to
repeat the dance. Cody, ready or not, led the way not seeming
to realize he had ever been there before. Mark saw me through.
After my night with Cody and Mark's night with Freddy, Mark
and I had our night with each other: sweet moments of unbelief
that I loved him and he loved me too. As the year wore on, as
our time together and our times in bed together added up to a
mutual history of understanding, I reached a point where I felt I
couldn't live without him. Mark had made me feel it was safe to
fall in love with him.

Mom and Freddy were not blind to my changes. They said
very little, most of what *was* said being uncritical, but I could
tell they were concerned, especially at my increasing absences
from school. I think Mom would have been more inclined to
intervene had she not been having so many problems of her
own.

One benefit to getting drunk with Cody was being able to discuss things with him we might have been too inhibited to discuss when sober. The most important of these topics, of course,

was how I felt about him. As it turned out, Cody brought the topic up himself, while we were sitting on a curb outside the Magic Theatre.

"Have you ever felt like you wanted to make love to me?" Cody asked. We had been discussing how someone up in Fayetteville had discovered that *Ronald Wilson Reagan* is an anagram for *Insane Anglo Warlord.*

I felt a dread go through me, probably not unlike what an escaped convict must feel when he hears a megaphone spout, "Come out with your hands up; we've got you surrounded."

"Why are you asking me this?" I said slowly, as calmly as I could manage.

"I'll explain in a minute, but first answer my question."

I shrugged, trying to seem casual. "Well, I've made love to you in my dreams several times."

"Mine too," Cody said.

I caught his eyes, his cheerful grin, wondering what he was getting at, why he had brought up the subject. I could think of one reason that would have made me very happy, but I wasn't going to jump to conclusions.

"What about when you're not dreaming?" Cody asked. "What about right now?"

That certainly changed the perspective. I took a sweeping look around the parking lot and decided to hell with it, I'd tell him anything he wanted to know.

"Sure, Cody, I'd like to make love to you. I mean, you've already become my best friend, and I'm happy just being friends with you. But there's this other attraction too. I like being close to you. I like it now sitting here beside you, and I like it when you sleep with me. To me it's almost like we're making love already because we're so close. But sometimes I think about having sex with you, and I wish we could give it a try."

"Those times I've slept over — why didn't you bring it up?"

"But what if you'd been repulsed or something? How could I risk it? Besides, you were drunk the last time, and it would have been taking advantage to mention it then."

"Yeah ... I understand. Thanks."

"Well, I've answered your question. So what were you going to explain?"

Cody sighed. "This is complicated. You see . . . I've never thought much about sex with another guy, not until you came along. But as soon as we met, I instinctively knew a lot about you, and one of the things I knew was that you . . . were interested in me physically."

I started to protest, but Cody stopped me.

"That's fine, you've already said as much, and that's why I wanted you to admit it before I told you this, so there wouldn't be any bullshit. Now listen. I've dreamed about making love to you, and in my dreams I enjoyed it a lot. I love you, Trotsky, and when I get affectionate with you it's because I love you and because I want to please you. But I like girls, I always have, and this is all new to me. I think I could get off having sex with you, but I could never feel the way you would about it. And that doesn't seem fair. I mean, I couldn't stand it if our relationship became one-sided like that. I always want to give you as much as you give me, and it scares me to think maybe I can't satisfy you."

There was a pause, for my response. I didn't give any, so Cody continued: "I just didn't want to deceive you. I've been worrying the last couple of days that my touching you all the time might make you start wondering if I'm gay. You make me wish I were, but I can't change that. I'm sorry."

There was another pause, but this time I had something to say. "You're the only person who's ever apologized to me for being straight," I told him. "If you want to know the truth, in my entire life I've had sex with just one person, so I don't know much about what I like best. But I've tried with girls before and it never worked. The attraction just isn't there."

"It's no big deal," Cody assured me.

I accepted his summation with a smile. I couldn't help thinking he was probably wrong. It shouldn't be a big deal, that was certainly true. Unhappily, I felt sure it would be.

Cody stood up, then lent a hand to help me to my feet. We walked back into the bar, ready for another round.

Ten

I had not seen much of Sarah or Flipping since the accident. Sarah was still in the hospital, where she had made it sufficiently clear she did not wish to receive visitors. She had taken Christian's death pretty hard. I hated hospitals anyway, and had been to see her exactly once. Sarah said she'd call me when they released her.

Flipping had stayed out of school for two weeks following the accident. Then, without telling either Cody or me, he had moved out of the Loft, dropped out of school, and gone to Natural Steps to live with his folks. I saw him only rarely, but frequently enough to know he was making a difficult passage.

On one occasion Flipping's parents had phoned to ask if I'd seen him. I hadn't, but later found out he'd been camping for several days by the LaFave River. He told Cody he needed time by himself to think.

Whenever he did get together with us, Flipping seemed hauntingly strange. He was smoking grass much more than before, and it was often hard for us to understand what he was talking about. Sometimes I would catch him staring at me with the blankest expression imaginable. I couldn't look into his eyes for long — the pain would come charging out and overwhelm me.

Still, Flipping could be animated and thoroughly entertaining from time to time. There is a brief stage of the marijuana experience when everything clicks together, when you become someone else, someone better at coming up with the perfect comment to get the spontaneous laugh. Flipping was able to regain this at times, but it never lasted the night, ultimately leaving him more depressed than ever. I knew Cody was getting frustrated, it was so difficult to talk to Flipping, so hard to be close to him. Finally, in a moment of exasperation, Cody accused him of preferring drugs to people. Flipping, silent for a long time, quietly stood up and left.

One weekend I decided to pay Flipping a visit. Before I really knew what was happening, I had agreed to take Cody, Freddy and Mark along with me. I actually wanted to see Flipping alone, but it turned out to be a good thing I had company. When we arrived, Mr. Benning told us Flipping was running some errands, but should be back in about two hours. It seemed a long time to wait, but Mr. Benning suggested we saddle up the horses for a ride, an idea that appealed to Freddy and Mark at once.

There were still only three horses in riding condition, so Mark doubled up with Freddy, later switching to ride with me. Freddy was having some problems getting back in the hang of things. He had gone riding with me only a few times in Nebraska, an experience already grown remote. At any rate, Freddy thought he could do better on his own, which proved to be the case. He was on the black stallion I'd ridden last time, since I knew it was a good, tame horse. Cody was again on the palomino, and I was on a stubborn, skewbald mare.

Mark had never ridden before, so when he joined me in the saddle I handed him the reins, then told him in five minutes everything I knew about riding. I tried to keep the horse at a walk until Mark got used to being up on a saddle. The nag was not especially cooperative, wanting to trot, but eventually I got her to do what I wanted. With the horse in line, I was able to concentrate more on Mark. We were not talking much today. As the sun was unseasonably hot and we had long ago begun to sweat, I could feel the wetness from Mark's back penetrating the two shirts and mixing with the moisture on my chest. His brown shirt, stretched tight across his shoulder blades, was tucked snugly inside his jeans, accenting his slender, tapered waist.

When we reached a clearing, I asked Mark for the reins and immediately nudged the horse into a canter, and then a run — something she was particularly fond of doing (the problem was getting her to stop). In front of my face, just below my nose, Mark's hair was lifting and falling to the gallop, catching the sun's rays in a dazzling array of blindness and sight, bringing his beautiful neck partially into view every third hoofbeat. When we were far enough from Cody and Freddy, I held the reins with one hand while possessing Mark's waist with the other, catching a soft, vaguely masculine scent I had smelled before, some unique, individual fragrance that was Mark when he perspired. I returned the horse to a walk, then handed Mark the reins, kissing him quickly below the ear before Cody and Freddy caught up with us, demanding to know what the hell we thought we were doing, where the hell we thought we were going.

After three and a half hours, Flipping had not shown up. Mr. Benning was a mixture of anger and anxiety as he apologized. Cody assured him we understood, we all thanked him for letting us ride the horses, then we were back in my car, heading down a highway that still produced a chill.

Mom had begun to receive some very nasty letters, some containing threats directed not only toward her, but also toward Freddy and me. The police were notified but seemed disconcertingly reluctant to pursue the matter.

One day I arrived home from school to find a band of evangelists camped in front of our house, protesting our "ungodly" family. At first I thought it was funny, but it got to be annoying soon enough. If they had been content to hold their signs and remain quiet, it wouldn't have been so bad. Late in the afternoon, however, they began to sing hymns, stomp around, and clap their hands. One or two even began speaking in tongues, after which a starchy old woman with a bellowing voice delivered an "interpretation," in which "God" called upon his people to rid his land of pestilence. I guessed this god of theirs was Jehovah, that they considered themselves to be his people, Arkansas his land, and the Trottingham-Taylors, sure as the devil, to be the pestilence. I had watched them briefly through the curtain in Freddy's room before starting on my homework. With all their muckraking, it was they who proved pestilential, making it impossible for me to concentrate on my lessons. Luckily, we had neighbors, who soon phoned the police to complain. After an hour of arguing with the cops, the Christians disbanded.

"Have you thought about moving?" I asked Mom later in the evening.

"Do you mean running away?" she asked me right back.

"No. I mean moving."

"Do you not like it here?"

"It's not that, it's just that I'm getting tired of all the hassles."

"Well . . . ," she said slowly, "if it gets to be too much, you tell me and we'll work out something. I'm not leaving. I am right about this, and I won't move away and let the wrong side win. But I have thought about you and Freddy, of course. It's not right for you to have to go through this, because it's not your battle. I've called your Aunt Lillian in Milwaukee, and I've phoned the Bayers in Lincoln. You and Freddy could stay at either place until this is over — just say the word."

"I would never go back to Lincoln. And I wouldn't leave you here by yourself, you know that. Besides, I believe you're doing the right thing. I just feel like these people can hurt us if they want to, and some of them are acting like they want to."

She was silent for some time. "It's funny," she said. "You have one of the poorest states in the country, a state whose people would benefit most from the economic policies I believe in, yet they see me as their enemy. I think it's all connected with some misconception they have that socialists are anti-Christian.

You can make them work long hours and pay them just enough to get by, you can take their sons and send them overseas to get killed so the multinationals can turn a bigger profit ... but you can't mess with their religion."

"A powerful opiate," I agreed.

"More like amyl nitrite. It seems to knock them silly and kill every brain cell God gave them. I'm not giving up, Trotsky. I think Arkansas may have a brighter future than a lot of places. The people here possess some qualities that are essential to society. They're hard-working, and many of them are willing to help each other out."

"You know, that day when Cody and I went to hear you lecture, I was really proud of you. I kept sitting there thinking how you and Dad both devoted your lives to humanity, and how that sort of unselfishness is exactly what I admire most in people."

"Don't give me too much credit, Trotsky. Your father was the dedicated servant of humanity. I just tried to do my job and ended up on the front page."

"But you hold all the right values, and you stick to those values. You help the cause of mankind every day just by *thinking* the way you do. When I think of some of the people out there who could have raised me, I wonder why I was fortunate in getting the parents I did. I mean, I never even knew Dad, yet his life was so special the mere *legend* of my father has been a guiding force to me. I'd rather have that legend of a father with me than any of these flesh and blood camels living their lives in bad faith."

Mom laughed. "Who have you been reading? Nietzsche or Sartre?"

"Okay, okay, so I mixed metaphors! But do you see my point?"

"Of course. And it pleases me to hear you speak so well of your parents."

I felt embarrassed, and I imagined she did, too.

"Actually I've been reading Berdyaev."

"Ah! The Russian who thought nature was overrated. Nicolai Berdyaev — I haven't come across his name since college. I'm surprised you know of him."

"It was pretty much an accident. I was looking through a book of existentialist philosophers and something Berdyaev wrote about free will caught my attention."

"Do you remember what it was?"

"Yes, it was something about free will traditionally being a source of man's enslavement. Man was told he had free will, but if he didn't exercise it in the choice of 'good,' he would be punished. Berdyaev believed freedom could lead to evil as well as good. I remember he said moral life is a tragedy, and this makes ethics the philosophy of tragedy. That struck me as similar in theme to all the talk about Abraxas in Hesse's *Demian* — Abraxas being the god that encompasses both good and evil."

"Could you worship such a god?"

"No, evil and decadence have never appealed to me. I'm attracted to honesty and innocence, which is pretty old-fashioned of me, I realize, but that's where my affections lie. On the other hand, I could never accept a god who gives his creatures free will only to punish those who do not choose the 'correct' path. If a god provides a spectrum of choices, he should honor them all. It isn't the way I would have set up a world, but whatever god we're dealing with, assuming there's one at all, has created one hell of a varied spectrum of lifestyles, different stimuli eliciting different responses, a cause-and-effect wonderland for someone who likes to study possibilities. I think that must be our god."

"Sounds as if you've thought it through rather well."

"How can you help but think about it? It's the only thing I've thought about for the last two years: *Why the hell am I here?*"

"Do you ever blame me for putting you here?"

"Well, not really blame you. But I have wondered before what you could have possibly been thinking. Did the world seem so much better eighteen years ago you thought I would en-

–153–

joy it? Did you enjoy the experience so much that you thought it generous to pass it on?"

"There was a bit of that. And parents are selfish, too. They have children simply because they want them. It makes you feel more important to have someone around who truly needs you, someone you can influence in a major fashion and control in a very direct way."

"It's hard for me to believe those were your reasons."

"Don't kid yourself, some of that was there. But you're right, my major reason for having you was your father. He desperately wanted children, so I guess the question really is what on earth *he* was thinking. But your father was just the sort of optimistic person who probably thought you would enjoy it. And if he'd been around, maybe you would have."

"It hasn't been that bad."

"You worry too much about my feelings. I'm not hurt, believe me."

"What about Freddy? What were you thinking then?"

"With Freddy, I simply thought you should have a brother or sister, someone to grow up with." She paused. "No, that's not true. Truth is, it was pretty much a case of rape. Freddy's father and I were on the verge of breaking up, then suddenly I was pregnant again. I didn't want to be pregnant, but I was. I thought about an abortion, but even though I've always supported a woman's right to make that choice, I couldn't choose it for myself. It was a Sartrian choice if ever there was one ... I put off making the decision for so long that eventually it was too late and the choice was made for me."

"Well, I'm glad there's a Freddy."

Mom smiled. "He *is* pretty special."

There was a pause, until I said, "It would be cruel bringing a child into the world now, the way things are."

"Doesn't sound like I'll be getting any grandchildren from you."

"No. I don't know. I don't think so."

Another silence followed. I could tell from studying Mom's

face that there were several questions she was considering asking me, and was looking at me for permission to ask. Something in my eyes gave her that permission.

"Is Cody your lover, Trotsky?"

My heart turned somersaults at the directness of the question, but I tried to stay calm as I answered.

"I've often wished that were true. And he's even told me *he* wishes it were true. But no, his affections don't run that way. Cody's straight."

Mom grimaced. "I'm sorry, it's just that all these labels people use to pigeonhole affections make me wince. Saying Cody's straight makes it sound as if he's either dead or wearing a heavily-starched shirt."

"I know what you mean. I'm not too thrilled with the opposing labels, either."

"Ignore them. They're only words."

"I try my best."

"Do you suppose this difference in you and Cody has anything to do with free will?"

This time I had to laugh. "Like choosing your hair color? Surely you must know from your own experience that it doesn't."

"I think for some people there is an amount of free will in choosing sexual preferences. That's why those people call them 'preferences.' But you're right — I think for the vast majority it's reduced to a matter of choosing to act on one's given sexual attractions, of choosing to be one's self."

Suddenly there was a loud crashing sound behind me, as a brick went hurtling by my head and knocked a lamp off an end table. I could hear the sound of squealing tires outside as a car sped away. We sat in silence, staring at the brick on the carpet.

I stood and picked it up. On one side was scribbled, "Commies burn." Without showing it to Mom, I took it into the garage and put it in a garbage can. Then I found some sheets of plastic and a spool of heavy-duty tape and went outside to see what I could do about the window for the night.

I had begun to look forward to Saturday nights as the highlight of my week, for Saturdays always meant Mark spending the night with Freddy, and Mark and me in bed. On the Saturday following the breaking of our window, I was awakened around noon when Freddy and Mark made a tentative entry into my room. Freddy was holding a small creature with long, pointed ears.

"It's a rabbit," he said.

For a moment I imagined myself to be in a maternity ward, having just given birth, when the nurse comes in holding a small, furry animal and announces quite cheerfully, "It's a rabbit!"

"I can see it's a rabbit," I said to Freddy. "But what's it doing in here?"

"Mark's dog caught it, but we got it away from him before he killed it. I'm gonna put it in the garage and see if I can fix it up."

They left, leaving me to contemplate my own bad humor. It was a pity anyone ever had to wake me up for anything. I was certainly the royal grouch. Freddy knew this. Obviously he wouldn't have awakened me unless he thought it was something important or something very special. I'm sure he wished now he hadn't. My fault — I'd make it up to him.

Cody came by soon afterward. I could hear Freddy warning him I was probably still asleep, then asking what we were going to do today.

"I don't know," Cody answered. "I thought I'd see if Trotsky has any ideas."

"That's being rather optimistic," Freddy said, as Cody opened the door to my room.

"What's eating Freddy?" Cody asked. "That's the first time I've ever heard him insult you."

"Oh . . . never mind. What's up?"

"Not you, pal. You gonna lay there all day or what?"

"Yeah, well, maybe if you'd turn your back or something, I might get up."

"Turn my back? I see you every day in gym, what'd'ya mean, turn my back?"

"Is this going to be an argument or what? *Just turn your back!*"

Instead, Cody just stared at me, grinning. Then he tried to throw the cover off me, but I held on tight.

"Who were you dreaming of?" he asked.

"You think I'm gonna say you, doncha?"

Cody didn't answer, but he at least gave up trying to uncover me.

"I just gotta piss. It's a hard-on from piss, all right? But never mind, you can see it if you want. If you don't want, then turn your head."

I got up and began to hunt through my closet for a pair of clean jeans. It was definitely time to do laundry. While shoving my legs through a pair I only wore when all others were too dirty, I heard Cody clicking on the stereo behind me.

"Let's play tennis," he suggested.

"I didn't know you played tennis."

"I don't much. Are you any good?"

"No, not much."

"Do you have two rackets?"

"Yeah, but I haven't used them in a long time, so I don't know what condition they're in."

"I'm sure they're as good as we are."

"Really! I'd hate to be outclassed by my equipment!"

It was a cold day, but at least there was no wind. We spent a lot of time chasing balls, and I was having problems with my jeans, which were too loose, but still clung to me as they crawled down my rear, taking my underwear with them.

"Do we change sides after the first game?" Cody asked.

"Yes. After all the odd games."

"Well, that was certainly an odd game."

I'd won, love–game, only because Cody double faulted four times straight. My serving was a little better, and we even had a few volleys. Then Cody got his serve in line, and the rest of the set went pretty well. The game kept reminding me of the status of our relationship. We'd really hit it off, but now it seemed we were just hitting it back and forth, happiest when the ball was in the other's court.

Our match was halted in the second set by a heavy rain. At first, when it was only a drizzle, we continued to play. But then a downpour began, thoroughly soaking us before we could make it to Cody's car. The drops were so big they stung when they hit your face.

"It's raining pigs and elephants!" Cody shouted as we slammed the doors in retreat.

He looked good, out of breath from the game and the run to the car, sweat and rain dripping from his hair down his face. His eyes were alive, his teeth perfect and bright.

"What does it feel like, looking like you?" I asked.

He froze for a moment in surprise, then honked his horn with a sudden slap at the wheel.

"I don't know. I mean, I think I'd already formed my personality by the time it dawned on me I was good-looking."

"Yes, but now, when you look in the mirror and you see this incredibly attractive face looking back at you, how does that feel?"

Cody smiled. "Trotsky, I expect this face stirs more emotion in you than it does in me. I just think of it as a very special gift, and one I've done nothing in this life to earn, which makes me wonder if maybe in some other life..." He stopped for a minute, then continued with a different thought. "But every gift carries with it a responsibility. I have the power, with my looks, to make people very unhappy, so I have to be careful."

"I think you handle it okay."

With the look Cody gave me, I could tell the tables were about to be turned, and I was the one who'd soon be grilled.

"And what's it like for you, Trotsky, being my friend but wanting to be more? When you look at me, does it make you happy or unhappy?"

I shifted my gaze to the puddles forming on the courts.

"There's not a face in the world I'd rather look at."

"Maybe I should repeat the question."

I sighed and pushed the wet hair off my forehead. The rain was letting up.

"It's raining gnats and fleas," I said.

Cody started the car.

Back at the house, I noticed how wet our clothes were and asked Cody if he'd like a change.

"No, your Mom's got a fire going. It won't take long to dry out."

I was anxious to get out of my slithering jeans, so I said, "Well, if you'll excuse me, I think I'll change into something less fluid."

Mark, who had been in Freddy's room, came into my room while I was changing.

"How's the rabbit?" I asked.

"He died."

"Oh."

Mark watched as I unzipped my jeans. "My mother wanted me and Freddy to stay at our house tonight," he said.

I was just removing the jeans, but stopped with one leg in and one leg out and looked at him in horror.

"Why? You're not, are you?"

"No, don't worry, I fixed it up. She thinks your house is too dangerous now, 'cause she'd heard about the broken window from a neighbor. But I told her Freddy and I always played his hockey set, and it wouldn't be any fun if we couldn't."

"Good thinking. Thanks a lot."

I was standing in my underwear now, and Mark came over to give me a nice warm hug before leaving.

"See ya tonight," he said.

I watched him as he closed the door.

Cody and I considered going out drinking, but couldn't get excited about that or any other idea. Besides, I was getting uneasy about going off and leaving Mom and Freddy by themselves. So, we joined Freddy and Mark for some hockey, agreeing it would probably be the best way to spend the evening. The game was set up in my room so we could listen to the stereo, then Freddy asked me to map out a round-robin tournament for the evening. This was simple enough: if we played each other twice it would make for a respectable tournament, and we more than likely would be sick of hockey by the time we finished.

There are many reasons why I will never forget this evening, and one of the most pleasant memories is the four of us together in my room playing hockey. I remember when Iggy Pop's "Lust for Life" came over the tape system, the game was halted while everyone sang along. I recall Cody winking at me as he sang the line about "something called love," and Mark inflecting his voice in some way to get my attention on the line about having "had it in the ear before."

None of us had much singing ability, but it was one of those moments when magic strikes the ordinary, making it oddly regenerative.

Cody asked if he could spend the night, and although I had been looking forward to stealing Mark out of Freddy's bed, there was no way I could refuse Cody. It was late before any of us got to bed, for after Freddy and I played a long, punishing championship game, we all had retired to the den and told stories from our pasts. I'm not sure exactly how long we were involved in this pursuit, but I had put a hefty log on the fire when we first went in the den, and it was nearly ashes by the time we left.

"It's been a good evening," Cody said later in my bedroom. "Those two kids are something else."

"They're fun to be around," I agreed.

"Yeah, I wish I could always have this much fun for free."

I began to undress while Cody looked through my tape collection to find the perfect tape to fall asleep by. He mussed my hair as I sat on the side of the bed removing my socks, then I climbed into bed while Cody began to undress. He turned off the light and crawled in beside me. We were both lying on our backs, hands under our heads, staring at the ceiling. It would have made an interesting photograph, I suppose, but at the time my thoughts were switching back and forth between Cody and Mark, wondering what Cody was thinking, and wondering if Mark would be lying awake waiting for me. We could go to the den, I was thinking, just as Cody propped himself up on an elbow to face me. My eyes met his, and I was surprised to see him looking rather serious, although he somehow managed to look a bit mischievous at the same time. His face began to come closer to mine, and as it did, he closed his eyes. Cody kissed me very politely on the lips.

"Can I just die now?" I asked him.

He smiled and circled my waist with his arms, drawing me toward him in something of a bear hug. Then we kissed again, only this time I felt Cody's tongue touch lightly against my lips, and I opened them to let it in.

I was confused, but didn't really want to form my confusion into a question just then. Cody took a finger and moved it along my chest. I searched his face, trying to find a trace of desire. I wanted nothing on earth just then so much as I wanted Cody to desire me, but somehow I felt his only desire was to do me a favor. He'd already told me he wasn't sexually attracted to guys, and I knew he wasn't lying when he said it.

"Don't you have problems finding sexual partners in Little Rock?" he asked.

For a moment I thought of Mark in the other room, and I thought of telling Cody. It might have saved us all a lot of trouble, but I didn't feel my confidence with Mark could be broken, even with Cody. And naturally, I was curious to know how this was going to turn out.

"I don't go 'round looking for it," I said. "But if I did, I doubt I would find it."

"Well," he said slowly. "You found me."

We let this statement float around the room a few times, with me wondering exactly what he meant, and Cody, I suppose, wondering how to explain it.

"I mean, I'm here ... I love you ... You love me ...

You're attracted to me . . . And, I mean, the idea of it doesn't repulse me. I can deal with it . . . For you, I can deal with it."

I was having a hard time thinking, for there were too many disjointed thoughts leaving me almost as soon as they came. I put enough of them together to say:

"It's too much to ask of you, Cody. It's not necessary, and it wouldn't be the same, knowing you really weren't into it."

Cody laid his head against my stomach. I could see his remarkable hair rise and fall with my breath.

"You wanna know something strange?" he asked.

"Sure." And I reached over to touch his hair and shoulder.

"Tonight I. . ." He raised himself to my face, to where his eyes were only inches from my own, and his lips were even closer. "Tonight I think I'm into it." And then he kissed me again, which was nice not only for the kiss, but because it altogether precluded my having to reply to what seemed the most important thing I'd ever heard. *He wanted me!* Or was he just trying to make it seem that way so I wouldn't feel guilty about his going along with it? He'd do that, I bet. . .

But I was feverish with excitement, and I'd given him every chance to back out of it.

So we made love, we made perfect our union, bodhisattvas not only in spirit and soul, but now physically bonded as well. And for the first time I experienced that taste in the mouth, that craving, that hunger for something born from the physical, but which itself is much more, something primal, seeking — what?

Cody kissed me again when it was over, and I knew then that this was the best, just being able to kiss him. He curled against my neck, presently settling into sleep. My thoughts turned again to the other warm body probably waiting for me in another room. Slowly and quietly, I slipped from Cody's grasp, got out of bed, grabbed my robe, and went to the bathroom. Then I made a stop in Freddy's room.

"Thought you weren't coming," I heard a voice say as I peered in through the darkness. "Want to use the den?"

He was standing beside me now, wearing only his underwear, and shivering slightly from the cold.

"Okay," I said. "I'll meet you on the couch."

I went back to my bedroom, making sure Cody was still asleep, and got a slip of paper from my chest of drawers. I had written a poem for Mark. In the den I pulled back a curtain just a bit so he could read it from the light of the corner streetlamp.

Virile and pulsing
full of movement,
full of life.
Three-fourths my age and
stealing my heart, you
are driving me off
the edge and
I love it.

Somewhere between mother's milk
and father's misplaced sanity you
struck truth head-on and
did not blink.

"What does 'virile' mean?" Mark asked me.

"Sexy," I told him.

"I like the part about my father."

It was quite true Mark's father was insane. I had run into him once or twice when I went over there to retrieve Freddy, and the man was a loony-tune if ever there was one. He was actually the main reason why Mark spent the night with Freddy a lot instead of the other way around. It was anybody's guess why Mark's mother continued to live with the man. I knew Mark didn't care for him in the least, and I had once heard Mark's younger sister say to her mother, "Mama, that man just drives me crazy." His primary pursuits appeared to be sleeping, cussing, belching, throwing beer cans through his bedroom window into the neighbors' yard, yelling at his kids, and accusing his wife of trying to kill him.

"I'm freezing!" Mark said, burrowing his head into my chest. I opened the robe and let him in.

"I love you, Mark."

He put his hands between my legs to keep them warm.

He looked better to me now than ever. Perhaps it was just that he was getting older, filling out more. Whatever the reason, it seemed the longer I knew him, the more attractive he became. I took my hand and ran it down his chest and stomach. He quivered slightly to the touch. Then I slipped my hand under his briefs. Mark slipped out of them and laid them aside. Of the dozen things I wanted to say, I couldn't begin to say anything. Instead, I moved my fingers around the moist area between his legs. We stared at each other even as we kissed. Mark closed his eyes and lifted his arms around my back, holding me in place, while I gently kissed his face, his eyelids, his cheeks, his forehead, and his neck. I held him like I had never held anyone, feeling every muscle in his body tighten, then feeling his teeth dig a little into my shoulder, not like our first time, but to suppress, pffff, a scream perhaps, as he gave me something valuable. Before Mark came along, I had forgotten what an early adolescent orgasm was like. Now, I often found myself wishing mine were still so intense. I often wondered, too, how I would have felt having a lover when I was fourteen. It was impossible to speculate, for I had difficulty remembering how I felt about anything when I was fourteen.

Mark seemed like a dead thing next to me, unable to move. I pulled his head onto my chest, hugging him tenderly, kissing his face. Within a minute, he was asleep in my arms. I knew it would not do for anyone to find us on the floor of the den together the next morning, since Freddy and Cody both knew where each of us had begun the night. Still, I put off awakening Mark for a long time, sleepy as I was, watching him sleep, timing my breathing to match his, smelling the somewhat musty smell of his hair next to my face. When I did wake him he apologized for falling asleep.

Climbing back into bed with Cody, the thing I kept thinking over and over was that too much had happened for one night; it was almost more than my mind could deal with. Looking back on it, I'm sure my mind could have dealt with the night just fine if it had ended then — if I had gone to sleep and woke up the next day with Cody beside me, with Freddy and Mark sleeping in the other room, their covers in the usual tangled heap at the foot of the bed, Freddy hugging his pillow to his chest as was his habit. But as a believer in the hills-and-valleys theory of life, I should have been on the lookout for valleys this night. If I had thought about it at the time, no doubt I would have looked upon Mom's tribulations at the university, the taunts at school and the brick through the window as valley enough, and the night's experiences with Cody and Mark as a well-deserved hill. But things can always get worse ... and what is a job, what are insults from strangers or a broken window when compared with your family, with your friends?

It must have been around four in the morning when Cody shook me awake. There was fear in the way he shook me, and there was terror on his face.

"Trotsky!" he screamed.

"What?"

But he didn't have to tell me what, for once awake, I could hear it, see it, for myself. The room was full of smoke, which my deficient nose was just beginning to detect, and from the other side of a wall was the roar of fire. I sprang to my feet at once, not bothering with clothes, ran to the door and opened it. Fire leapt in at me so fast it was all I could do to get the door shut again, not that it would keep the fire out for long.

Cody had slipped on some jeans and was working to open the window, which had swollen shut during the past month from all the rain and cold on the outside, heat on the inside. I thought of opening the door again, wanting to get to Freddy's room, to Mom's room, immediately, but had seen enough the first time to know I couldn't do it that way. I got my jeans on as Cody finally got the window ajar. I let him help me through it first, but didn't wait around outside to lend him any unnecessary assistance. I ran in a sweat to my mother's window, tried to open it, but of course it was locked. The fire had entered her room, and in the light of the flames I could see her lying on the bed. I wondered why she didn't wake up, then remembered that people die in fires from smoke inhalation. Perhaps it was panic, but the thought of her dying, the sight of the fire approaching her, was all I needed to make me crazy. I ripped at the window with anything I could find, mainly my own hands and fingers, until I broke it, unlocked it, unjammed it, and got it open. I was through in a flash, and within a second or two had lifted Mom out of the window, to Cody, who was standing outside. Once outside myself, I turned to run around the house to Freddy's room, but Cody put a hand on my shoulder to stop me. I looked at him for only a second, during which he shook his head, then I broke his grasp and ran around the flaming house, leaving Cody to see to Mom.

The fire obviously had started from the front, because the living room, the garage, and Freddy's room were already torched. I looked around me, searching for my life. There were neighbors everywhere, standing back at a safe distance. A fire truck was just arriving, an ambulance close behind. I looked once more at the house then ran to help Cody, who was carrying Mom away from the relentlessly raging flames.

Cody carried her to the ambulance himself. He looked desperate. He had been giving her mouth-to-mouth resuscitation, but she was not responding. A paramedic took over this task, while another person in a white suit tried to convince me I was bleeding dangerously, needed to get to the hospital. I looked at my hands, my arms. I hadn't realized. Then a fireman came running over, ordering the ambulance to wait. "We've got a burn victim!" the fireman shouted. "Found him trapped in the laundry room."

"There's two," I told him. "There should be two."

I heard a woman run screaming through the crowd. She was calling for her baby. She ran to the stretcher carrying the boy they found in the laundry room, then ran toward the flaming house, until a fireman grabbed her and pushed her back toward the crowd.

Freddy was lifted quickly into the ambulance, I was shoved in as well, then the ambulance went squalling through the streets of Little Rock, although it seemed we hardly were moving at all.

I didn't think Freddy was alive, saw absolutely no way he could be. On the way to the hospital they managed to revive Mom at least to the point where she was breathing regularly. They were making such a fuss with Freddy it finally dawned on me he must still be alive, or at least there must be some hope of reviving him, otherwise they wouldn't be making such an effort.

I kept thinking of Mark's mother, running toward the flames, screaming for her baby. My baby. Then I began to cry, to cry for all of us, to cry for shipwrecked humanity so bent on destroying itself. I didn't need the official reports the next day to know our house had been set afire deliberately. I had taken some of the calls myself, had read some of the letters, had picked up that blasted brick. Mom had chosen to believe they were bluffing. I had been satisfied with letting her make those decisions. Could I ever forgive her? Forgive myself? Of course I could. But I wanted so desperately to blame *something*, to believe in anything strong enough to lay some blame, be it god, devil or fate. But I could blame only a disease in human nature, and beyond that, only existence.

In my jeans pocket was the poem I had written for Mark and a polished shell Freddy had given me on my fifteenth birthday, which I'd grabbed off my window ledge as I crawled through.

At the hospital, several pieces of glass were removed from my arms and hands, then I received several stitches. As soon as the doctor was through, I went to see how the others were doing. Mom was just coming around enough to speak, and all she kept saying was, "Trotsky? Freddy?"

"I'm here," I said. She opened her eyes, but it was obvious she was having a hard time focusing. "Trotsky! Thank God! Is Freddy okay?"

"I'm going to check," I told her, and left the room. Walking down the hall to the burn unit, I thought about her barely-conscious words: "Thank God!"

I was told I could not enter the burn unit yet, so I sat down beside the door, waiting until I could. After an hour, Cody arrived, joining me on the floor.

"Your mother?" he asked immediately.

"She's okay. She was just coming to when I last saw her. That was about an hour ago, but they were giving her a sedative, so I imagine she's sleeping."

Cody looked partially relieved.

"Freddy's in there," I told him. "I haven't been able to see him."

We were silent for several minutes. I wanted to ask him, but I knew there was no hope. I couldn't bring myself to say the words.

"They couldn't put the fire out," Cody said. "So they just let it burn, made sure it didn't spread."

I nodded my head, to let him know I had heard.

"They found Mark. He was still in Freddy's room."

I tried to control it, found that I couldn't, then didn't care anymore. I buried my face in Cody's shoulder and cried like I had never cried before.

Some time later, a doctor came through the door, looking weary, his eyes bloodshot. "Are you Trotsky?" he asked. I said I was. "He's been asking for you. I think you could go in for just a few minutes, but don't stay long. I've got to get some sleep myself, but Dr. Leonard will be here in a few minutes to take over."

I appreciated the fact that Cody made no attempt to enter with me. I walked in, saw Freddy, and my eyes once again filled with tears. I walked up to the bed praying to anything that might help, to please let Freddy live.

"Trotsky?" I heard him say, in the tiniest voice I'd ever heard.

"Yes?"

"Is Mom okay?"

"Yes, she's fine. She's asleep now, but she's gonna be fine."

"Trotsky, did Mark . . . die?"

I didn't answer. What if I said yes and then Freddy died too? But I couldn't lie to him. Freddy opened his eyes as much as he was able. I could see he was crying, but something about the burns made it impossible for him to actually shed the tears.

"He wouldn't wake up," Freddy said. "Then I tried to run and get you . . . couldn't make it . . . couldn't make it back to Mark."

"Don't talk, Freddy! Please! Just rest for now, okay?"

The look on his face, in his eyes, was the most horrible expression of pain I have ever witnessed, and was more than I could bear to see on the face of my only brother. I felt myself collapsing, and the next thing I knew I was on my knees, kneeling beside his bed, wanting to embrace him but knowing I couldn't, and crying my heart apart, "Don't die Freddy! Please don't die!"

A nurse came in to check Freddy's pulse and temperature, and to give him a painkiller. She told me I shouldn't be in there, but I told her the doctor had said it was all right. She didn't look convinced, but left without a word. Freddy slowly lifted his hand off the bed for me to hold. "I love you," he said. With my free hand I reached in my pocket and retrieved the shell he had given me years earlier. I pressed it in his hand. Freddy did not exactly smile — I'm not sure that he could — but he looked pleased. And then he closed his eyes.

I knew at that moment I would never see those eyes again.

Eleven

Dawn came to the sandbar near Lock and Dam Number 7, where I had fled for lonesome refuge. Just to watch the river, to listen to its voice . . . if anything could help . . . but of course nothing could. It was essential I be alone, at least for a while.

I had stayed at the hospital only long enough to deliver the news to Mom myself. She was doped on something damn powerful, for I never was sure if she was understanding me. Finally, I couldn't stand to say the words another time, and turning to shrug helplessly at Cody, I literally ran for the hospital doors. Realizing I didn't have a car almost persuaded me to go back in for Cody, but instead I walked toward the river, then upriver toward the sandbar. On the way I heard the radio reports from the few cars parked at intersections waiting for lights to change, listening to the news of the tragedy in my life, my own private existence, now thrown open to the public at large. I resented that, and I couldn't bear thinking how a few people out there would be glad it happened.

Sitting on the sandbar, it surprised me how blank my mind had become, almost as if my brain had supplied its own anesthesia. Too numb to cry, I skipped rocks along the water, watched the sky get lighter as star after star disappeared before my eyes in unraveled mystery. I remembered the mythological explanations for dawn, tried to imagine living in a time like that, when Ra, the Egyptian sun-god, sailed unsuspectingly across the sky in his boat. Ra was dead now, but the sun still arose.

A city was coming to life around me, waking up to Sunday morning. In all the din of dissonance I picked out the sound of a single car engine slowly approaching. The engine stopped some distance behind me, at a point on the sandbar where cars could venture no further. I heard someone walk up behind me and sit down. I waited for the moment of silent communion to pass, then asked if my mother was doing okay.

"She's fine . . . except of course finding out Freddy . . . I waited around in case she needed me for anything, then they gave her another sedative and she went back to sleep."

I wondered how, in the end, she would face this pain. "Thank you for staying. I couldn't."

We sat there for perhaps an hour longer, until I felt I could go back to whatever was left to go back to. When I stood up, Cody caught me in an embrace into which we both poured every ounce of energy we had left. I felt the tension explode and collapse within me, then, emotion spent, I followed Cody back to his car. We drove to the hospital, finding Mom still asleep. Cody was feeling no desire to go home, and I no longer had a home, so we stayed at the hospital.

Within a few hours, flowers began arriving, too numerous to count, from people I didn't know. When there were more arrangements than could fit in Mom's room, a nurse asked me what should be done with the others. I had no idea, but Cody suggested the nurses gather the cards, then distribute the flowers to other patients who might appreciate them. This seemed like a good idea to me, and the nurse went away thanking us for our consideration. Later, I looked through some of the cards and discovered many were coming from members of the Democratic Socialists of America scattered across the country. Apparently the national news media had picked up the story quickly. I didn't care. I just wanted to wake up from one more nightmare, have Freddy shake me awake and tell me we'd be late for school. I still had the wrinkled slip of paper in my pocket with the poem I'd written for Mark — *Full of movement, full of life...*

I added the line to my collection of scars, those hurtful wounds which only time could diminish, as time made thistledown of my past. But I suspected humans had survived similar pains for thousands of years, and I expected I would survive mine as well, if I wanted to.

In the waiting room on that particular floor of the hospital, there was only one end of a couch unoccupied. Cody and I grabbed the empty space and collapsed there, not having slept in quite a while. As I felt myself drifting off, I leaned my head against his shoulder so I wouldn't accidentally fall on the poor man sitting beside me. Cody, slumped on the end, put his arm around me and shifted his weight to make my position more comfortable. Soon I was sleeping blissfully, not even troubled by dreams.

Perhaps due to my mother's popularity among certain members of the DSA (she had been one of the primary organizers of the party when it sprang from the New American Movement), or perhaps due to the legend of my father, socialists from across the country flocked to Little Rock, planning fund-raisers for Mom along with a massive rally in her support, protesting the tactics used by the Arkansas legislators, whom they held partially responsible for the nightmare. To a great extent, I shared their point of view. Furthermore, I found their sudden presence in Little Rock a blessing, for it kept Mom busy, and it kept both my mind and hers on things other than Freddy and Mark.

Meanwhile, the fire officially had been ruled an arson. Someone had doused the front of the house with gasoline and lit a match: a simple enough way to kill your enemies, real or imagined. The police claimed they had no suspects and possessed inadequate evidence to pursue an investigation. When the Democratic Socialists learned the police weren't even pursuing leads, they hired a private investigator, who gave them their money's worth. In less than a week he discovered who had set the fire, and within two weeks the evidence he had gathered forced the Little Rock Police Department to make arrests. The bond was ridiculously low, and the suspects were free within hours. A jury of their peers would later fail to convict them, and the state would decide not to appeal the verdict.

Our immediate problem of finding a place to live was solved by one of Mom's colleagues at UALR. A fellow economics professor had an apartment he rented out that recently had become vacant. He offered it to us free, but we persuaded him into accepting a minuscule sum each month until we were on our feet again. Things would be considerably better when the house insurance money came through. In the meantime, Cody helped out a bit by seizing the opportunity to officially switch families, moving into the apartment with us. We also received money from both the Trottinghams and the Taylors, so we got by all right. Although the apartment was in a different school district, Cody and I drove the seven miles across town each day and finished up the year at our old school.

On the day of the rally, upwards of five thousand people gathered at MacArthur Park in downtown Little Rock to march on the capitol. The permit had been denied at first, but the DSA and the ACLU had put together a good team of lawyers. They were able to get a permit only a day after the original request was turned down. DSA members from all over the country were converging on the park. There were a lot of Arkansawyers there as well, some of them socialists, some of them people who simply were appalled by what had happened.

Mom did nothing to encourage the rally, feeling the issuance of parade permits for political purposes was not a constitutional right, considering the expense involved.

"The Constitution guarantees the freedom of peaceful assembly," I heard her say to a DSA organizer, "not the right to parade down Capitol Avenue and insist the city pick up the tab."

Too, her heart just wasn't in it. And neither was mine. Cody made an appearance and filled me in on all the details not making the six o'clock news.

Sarah called a few days later, asking me to come see her. I found her sitting on the living room couch, decked out in something vaguely resembling the flag of North Korea. Although still wearing a neck brace, she looked surprisingly well. Conversation was awkward at first, but once we were comfortable with each other, it was amazing the things we were able to say. Upon returning home, I immediately wrote this poem:

> Me and Sarah, we ain't
> got no ambition,
> ain't even no motivation
> to be found.
> I kinduv like
> to have Sarah around.
> She and I, we
> real good friends.
> Hope to stay that way.
> She says that I don't bother her.
> One of the few, she say.
> Me and Sarah, we ain't
> wantin to die or nothin.
> Just sometime wish we never born.
> But if ya know the meanin of nothin,
> you can throw dice
> into an Alpine snowstorm.
> Me and Sarah, we
> somewhere above the norm.

I sent the poem to her a few days later, the same day I received a letter from Flipping, postmarked Los Angeles, telling me of his departure from Little Rock. He had decided to seek out musicians on the West Coast, uncertain when or if he would return to Arkansas.

I could tell Cody was floored when he read the letter. Aside from not knowing Flipping had left, I knew he was hurt that the letter had come to me instead of him.

"L.A. is expensive," Flipping wrote. "And I didn't have much money to bring with me. But I'm hoping the city's rolling in money and won't need mine."

Handing the letter back to me, Cody said, "My experience with people in the money is they want yours anyway."

There was no return address on the envelope, and I never heard from Flipping again. Although I could have called the Bennings and asked if they had his address, I did not.

Cody and I shared a room, shared a bed, for the remainder of the school year. We often preferred making love above the waist, with hearts and minds, arms and lips, but frequently explored the sub-navel regions as well. As the months flew past, that unfathomable bond between us seemed to mellow as the lasting tenets of our friendship sealed. That is, what once manifested itself in bizarre dreams and astounding coincidence began to manifest itself in more subtle ways — we could communicate everything that was necessary with a simple nod of the head, a certain look in the eye or curl of the lip. Our friendship had reached a level of spirituality I had encountered previously only in books. I never had any doubt Cody was basically straight except for his sexual encounters with me, but then I was basically celibate except for my experiences with him. Occasionally something he did would bring back a haunting recollection of Mark, and every time I see Mark in my mind, I see him so well I get depressed. I see him so well I explode inside and have to write it down . . . His eyes, his ear-to-ear smile, that blond mop of hair always falling in his face, the plain silver chain he wore around his neck, with the strip of leather resting on his chest . . .

And in time it was Cody whom I saw only as a memory, for life does go on, much longer than is necessary in some cases, and eventually our paths diverged.

Freddy, little brother, I am drunk with loneliness.

Mom is living in Milwaukee again. After winning a lengthy court battle which awarded her reinstatement and back pay, she declined the reinstatement, took the money and ran. I left Little Rock long before the case was settled, choosing to go to college at the University of Wisconsin in Madison. Cody stayed in Little Rock, dropping out of UALR after his sophomore year to work full-time for his girlfriend's father. Sarah probably still sees him occasionally. I wrote her a letter as soon as I got to Madison. Besides being my most faithful correspondent, she was also my last contact with Little Rock, and aside from Mom, the last person to call me "Trotsky."

Cody sent letters for a while, then for a longer while he would call from time to time and apologize for not writing, but make up for it with a good hour of conversation. Then there were Sarah's letters ending with "P.S. Cody sends his love." And after a time the message changed to "Cody says hello." From the time Cody met his girlfriend, Sarah didn't see him much, hardly mentioning him in her letters at all. Finally, the letters between us grew so thin in substance the line snapped.

The dreams had stopped long before, and in time all the strange occurrences began to seem like dreams themselves, or as if I'd imagined them. Was I ever that in tune with mysticism? In any case, I no longer feel those special powers working through my life, nor do I see people much these days. Like those jaded souls who become famous in their youth, who lose themselves to their own success, I wonder whom I could ever find to equal the sort of brother I had in Freddy, the lover I had in Mark, the friend I had in Cody.

If I saw Cody today I would ask him if he still believed in bodhisattvas, attaining nirvana but staying behind to help others. Or if, like me, he had found that the loss of desire does not lead one to nirvana, it only leads one to the doorstep of *nada*.

Freddy, little brother, I am drunk with loneliness. I follow my love like a demanding child, through the silence of Cody, through visions of Mark. But I come to you when my heart is breaking. When I need goddamn anything to live, to remain a force on earth, I come to you.

Coda

From the notebooks
of Steven Trottingham Taylor
and Washington Damon Cody

I look through old notebooks.
I laugh again
at you striking out my capital "G" gods
for little ones of your own.

You claimed our meeting was designed;
predetermined by the moon or
the Masons or the woman who spooked you
the night before.
Our convergence was poetry: A merger
of insanity with illusion.
For friends you gave totality;
Time, for the patience of old souls;
Mind, for the loss of thought;
Faith, for the history of humankind;
Body, for the tryst of affection.

You claimed we had destiny.
Looking back,
I'm sure we believed it.
Things happen.
I'm sure it could be truth.
I suppose it could still be true.

Your essence was khaki madness,
scrambled with the best of souls
from Renaissance men.
Believers in each other,
Bodhisattvas linked to a common soul—
we saw it as a mirror.
Yes, we had destiny.

(STT)

♣

I keep moving as I stand motionless.
Ear for love.
Senses ponder the fate you and I share.
Only some old Buddha up there
truly knows the effects.

(WDC)

❧

A dream above a Cody creation: My denim God.

Middle part of morning — yawning yourself awake. I could
    not.
I knew time waited only for me. The world was not involved.
A moment pitting me against a soft grey eternity.
I had slept in pajamas, first time in years.
Chilling cold. No heat, no heaters. Too much white.
This was an overdeveloped dream. I tried to steal a pillow. . .
Wisconsin came to mind. Gut of the midwest. *Nada.*
There was something about those icebergs resting against her
    side,
when Time waited only for Wisconsin. A land to grow.
The dream was planted: My denim god and a baby continent,
too old for that now. A seascape to deface.
My hands on arms still thrashing. One hard shove, that iceberg
    be gone
Forever. One deep thrust. This time ا
This time
     This
  This   time I
        CONNECTED
with the pillow and the light began to fade.
I shook with internal applause. Time gave a nod, moved on.
The day began to take shape, as I pulled away.
I hovered in the void of the morning, over what was once my
    bed,
or maybe what was me. I hovered there, a dream above a
    strange
stretch of space. I began to rise, but it felt like
sinking
into a dream of a Cody creation: My denim god.

                                    (STT)

❋

The Magic Theatre: Hesse's coal mine

No more cork in the open sores,
Madmen stationed at every door,
Dragons springing up out of the urinal,
more Loch Ness than not.
Graffiti dancing nude on the makeshift stage,
Dancers nailed to the walls of the mine shaft wage.
But it all comes
    down
to table legs and
    toes,
collapsable cups in the vacant hours of morning,
I giving shadow boxer mute fair warning.
No ear
for the taste of victory here.

                            (WDC)

♣

Mercy, Those American Boys

Their nicknames making good album titles,
engraved in their minds: autobiographies,
better than Gide's,
somewhat better than the letters setting Africa free.
They toy with the spirit of the Huck Finn vision.

Cody memorized Psalm 95...
                    the memory lingers on...
Home again, feeling safe with sin,
he resurrects the body of his riverboat friend.
They fade away in neon, barefoot crost a continent
        too old for them now.

        Two minors, unsteady, and conspiring to erupt.
        (No minors left for Majors to corrupt.)

Kept awake with tension, Trotsky watches Cody sleeping:
naked to the morning, head beneath a pillow,
the tan that looked so good the night before
        looking wasted now.
Cody sleeps away the day until the sun goes down,
then getting up and putting on his blues and browns,
he says, "That domino theory really works, Trotsky."

Cody in pieces, like most interlocking males,
tries to be happy,
fails, tries, fails.
Huckleberry smokes seven Camels every hour
as he and Tom wander through a country gone sour.
He sketched their epitaph in the Arkansas clay.
Tom wrote it on the mirror in lipstick today.
It said: "Life don't work."

And then he
crossed it out.

Mercy, those American boys.
Breathing love into each other,
taking life from one another—
stuck in place

A day
in space
means nothing to them now.

(STT)

♣

Floored and Floorboard, More Bored Oh Lord

The day Time stood stilted,
all the humming stopped.
The cosmic hum, the death hum,
the hum of vacancy—
ceasing suddenly and invocationally,
People clapped hand to ear,
fingers groping around the wax.
        "Hey, hey,"
the synapse is on the blink,
        "so this is the way
        you felt in Lincoln,
        so this is the way
        to the Sartrian haunt...

"I left a sigh of belief
on your bureau.
You'll see it, waking,
if that's what you want."

                    (WDC)

♣

Burning on the ropes
with the Buddha just a chant away
Terminal dreams and aspirations
are tied into the abyss
self-inflicted through bad faith
and burning on the ropes.

I can remember once
when I almost became this river
I sought to know her currents
her depths, her sediments...
her powers and faith.
I tell you, I almost became this river.
Her depths and sediments
Burning on the ropes.

Illuminous fragments of blessings
from the supernova of a far removed god
make Her indifference our frustration,
turn our fates to straw.
Too many people for Him to handle.
Too many crimes for Her to care.
Too many prayers for It to hear.
Too many   Too many   Too many
fates turned into straw
and burning on the ropes.

                                    (STT)

                    ♣

Transformer

Stencil butterflies fluttering their ink
align antennae, hung over from transformer days:
twin toxic rays,
Thorax and abdomen, clothed in drag,
soak the sunlight, then at night,
nocturnal cousins streak the dark,
in search of Light.
Lunas lashing with the waves, pursuing, crashing.
Human mammals slap and scratch
their barren flesh, with plans to hatch.

(WDC)

They lean on walls, virgules to the graffiti.
Jehovah's witnesses, they
been called to the stand.
Paramount to oblivion, isosceles with the buildings.
Is there hope for humankind?
Or does this hope choose certain individuals?
Faith beyond reason, captured and preserved
in smooth young bodies
checking my oil in Little Rock, Arkansas
(Man, that ain't mascara, that's grease),
with a rag in one hip pocket,
and *Siddhartha* in the other.
     There is hope for humankind
     (condensed in the individual).

(STT)

Their words metamorphosed on their lips
slide down their chins, frail sinking ships.
(But some small few, accused of dreams,
 tolerate the plans, tolerate the ships,
 tolerate intolerance in other men.
 Frail stencil seers search through the years:
 Some hope for humankind lies here).

(WDC & STT)

❧

What do you do with a boy who says damn?
(The Restoration)

Tarot kindergarten angels
of missionary myths
whisper tales their mothers told them
in Holy Roller tongues
of themselves when they were mortal
and wanted to die young.

"My friend, the dragon, told me
he had a death wish once,
but met a dragon-lady
whose love kept him alive.
He said it takes
one friend, at least,
for humans to survive.
I wonder if I'd had a friend
if I'd have come to this. . .

His friend, an angel, hushed him,
and answered with a kiss,
"Only some fool bodhisattva
would force existence on a friend."

The kindergarten angels
forced themselves to quite agree.
Trotsky, they must like you,
but they'd rather play with me.

(WDC)

✿

Stay Gold

I remember friends like brothers
when friends were what you lived for.
I remember friends always there,
to live your life with.
I remember friends who knew every secret,
when friends loved you for everything you were.

Then it was you and me cause we
were in this crazy wreck together—
that being what we had.

It was everything.

It was that gripping fear
that even the closest of friends grow apart.

(STT & WDC)

Other books of interest from
ALYSON PUBLICATIONS

★ REFLECTIONS OF A ROCK LOBSTER: A story about growing up gay, by Aaron Fricke, $6.00. When Aaron Fricke took a male date to the senior prom, no one was surprised: he'd gone to court to be able to do so, and the case had made national news. Here Aaron tells his story, and shows what gay pride can mean in a small New England town.

★ EXTRA CREDIT, by Jeff Black, $6.00. Harper King's life consists of a boring job, stagnant relationships, and a tank full of fish named after ex-lovers, dying in the same order their namesakes were seduced. Now he decides he wants a fresh start in life — but life doesn't always cooperate.

★ THE TWO OF US, by Larry Uhrig, $7.00. The author draws on his years of counseling with gay people to give some down-to-earth advice about what makes a relationship work. He gives special emphasis to the religious aspects of gay unions.

★ COMING OUT RIGHT, A handbook for the gay male, by Wes Muchmore and William Hanson, $6.00. The first steps into the gay world — whether it's a first relationship, a first trip to a gay bar, or coming out at work — can be full of unknowns. This book will make it easier. Here is advice on all aspects of gay life for both the inexperienced and the experienced.

— — — — — — — — — — — — — — — — —

Enclosed is $_____ for the following books. (Add $1.00 postage when ordering just one book; if you order two or more, we'll pay the postage.)

1. _____

2. _____

3. _____

name: _____

address: _____

city: _____ state: _____ zip: _____

ALYSON PUBLICATIONS
Dept. H-5, 40 Plympton St., Boston, Mass. 02118